Richard Benson, returning to his place on the plane, saw that the seats his wife and daughter Alice had occupied were vacant. He beckoned to the stewardess who, minutes before, had shown them their seats.

"Is my wife all right? She's not back there sick, is she?"

"Your wife?" said the stewardess, frowning a little.

"Yes. She isn't ill from the plane motion, is she? Or the little girl?"

"I don't understand," said the stewardess.

Benson's gray eyes flamed through her. "My wife and daughter," he said distinctly. "The woman and the little girl who were sitting in those two seats in front of mine."

"Those two seats were vacant," said the stewardess.

JUSTICE INC.

by Kenneth Robeson

NEW YORK

Prologue

In the roaring heart of the crucible, steel is made. In the raging flame of personal tragedy, men are sometimes forged into something more than human.

It was so with Dick Benson. He had been a man. After the dread loss inflicted on him by an inhuman crime ring, he became a machine of vengeance dedicated to the extermination of all other crime rings.

He turned into the person we know now: a figure of ice and steel, more pitiless than both; a mechanism of whipcord and flame; a symbol of destruction to crooks and killers; a terrible, almost impersonal Force, masking chill genius and supernormal power behind a face ever as white and dead as a mask from the grave. Only his pale eyes, like ice in a polar dawn, hint at the deadliness of the scourge the underworld heedlessly invoked against itself when crime's greed turned the retired adventurer, Richard Henry Benson, into—The Avenger.

CHAPTER I

Vanished!

Under the May sun, the Buffalo airport looked as peaceful as a pond in a calm. Like a pond it had its water bugs—planes, some standing, one coming onto the runway, several wheeling into position for a take-off.

Calm and peaceful in the late May sun. Looking back on it, Richard Benson found it almost impossible to realize that in that peace and orderliness had begun the fantastic thing of horror that was to change the whole course of his life.

Such things couldn't grow from a germ of terror nesting in that peaceful spot. Such things couldn't happen anyway! Not to Benson, who was known by all his friends as the luckiest man they knew.

But the seed of tragedy did sprout from that field. And the thing did happen to him.

A ten-passenger Douglas was one of the two planes with props idling for a getaway. It squatted on the runway receiving the last luggage of passengers into its maw. And Benson saw it from the window.

Benson was talking to the agent.

"I've got to get to Montreal at once! You understand? I've got to!"

The agent was listening respectfully. People always listened respectfully to Benson. His jet-black hair, framing a lean, square face, his pale-gray eyes, flaming with vitality and will, his erect, whipcord body and swift, sure movements, inspired respect on sight.

But just the same the agent shook his head.

"The Montreal plane leaving now is booked solid. Didn't they tell you at the downtown office?"

Benson's eyes were like pale-gray fire.

"They told me. But there *has* to be a place for the three of us. My wife's mother is dying in Montreal."

He put his hand—the kind of slim-fingered, long hand that is made up of steel wire and leather sinew—on the arm of Mrs. Benson, who added mute appeal to his out of soft brown eyes.

She was beautiful. Benson's wife. Tall and lovely and slim, with soft gold hair and dark-brown eyes. She looked like a gold-crested gray dove in her tweed traveling suit. Benson's face softened as he looked at her. It always did. And the hard flame in his gray eyes always softened when they rested on the dainty little figure beside Alicia Benson—his little daughter, as brown-eyed and gold-haired as her mother. A wife and girl to be proud of, those two!

The agent was shaking his head, looking sympathetically at the three.

"It simply can't be done. There's a plane at midnight—"

"Can't wait that long," snapped Benson. His face was a lean square of inflexible purpose. There was on it the look that had come there in his varied and adventurous past, when some problem unsolvable to ordinary men came up—and was solved by him.

"I'll charter a plane. I don't care how big—"

"We haven't a plane on the field to be chartered," said the agent. "I'm afraid you simply won't be able—"

It was then that Benson looked out the airport office window and saw the Douglas wheeling to the runway.

Without a word to the agent he hurried to the door, with Alicia and little Alice coming after him.

"What are you going to do, darling?" Alicia Benson asked. Her voice was as lovely as the rest of her. In it was implicit trust in this gray flame of a man.

8

"I'm going to get us to Montreal at once if I have to—"

The banging door shut off his sentence. He hurried to the airliner.

At rest Benson compelled respect. In motion he roused something like awe. Only about once in a decade do you see a man move with the flow of easy power, the perfect co-ordination and the rhythm of intense vitality owned by Richard Benson. Yet he didn't look particularly big. He was no more than five feet eight, weight about a hundred and sixty.

He and Alicia and little Alice got nearly to the plane. The double metal door was still open, the stairs still in place. An attendant came around the plane and stood in front of them.

"You the three who have the vacant seats on this plane?" the attendant asked.

He was tall and bony, with knobs of hands and with red, coarse skin. Sandy eyebrows were like sand ropes over his frosty blue eyes.

Benson stared at the man, eyes pale blazes of triumph.

"So there are three seats on that plane! Everybody said there was no chance to board her. Perfect conspiracy to keep us from getting aboard! But we'll show 'em."

"If you haven't the tickets—" the attendant began, with a heavy Scotch burr.

"We'll pay at the other end. Fix up the irregularity any way you please. Come on, sweethearts."

Up the steps and into the plane. A roar of the props, slam of the metal door, which was locked into place, and then motion. And Benson looked around. He was doomed right then, though he didn't know it.

There were six men and a woman in the plane besides the Bensons. The woman was young, pretty, but with a hard line around her mouth. One of the men was big and flabby with surplus flesh; another was big, but not flabby, and had pads of black hair on his hands; a third was short and stout, and chewed an unlit black cigar. The other three were just average, to be lost in a crowd.

9

"Comfortable, honey?"

Benson leaned forward in the seat and laid his hand on his wife's shoulder. A perfect union was advertised in every movement of these two.

"I'm fine, don't worry," smiled Alicia Benson. And little Alice piped up, "I'm fine, too, daddy."

Benson relaxed, body moving easily to the slight motion of the plane. Off to the west, at their tail, the late sun dipped under the horizon and purple dusk capped the landscape.

They were on a visit to a deathbed; but Alicia's mother was old, and death comes gently to the aged. In spite of their errand, Benson could not help but feel almost happy as he dwelt on the great good fortune that was his.

He had the world by the tail—or so it seemed as the grim purple dusk lowered. A perfect family, a large fortune to lavish on them, comparative youth, and health—

The plane roared east and north. Underneath, the ebon surface of Lake Ontario was a black steel sheet under a starless sky. The short, stout man chewed his dead cigar and stared expressionlessly at Benson and the softly beautiful woman and the little girl. The big man with the pads of black hair on the backs of his hands looked out the window, paying no attention to anyone.

The stewardess, a girl of twenty or so, slim and attractive in the airline uniform, bent over Mrs. Benson to ask if she and the little girl were all right. And Benson got up, rubbing his hands together. They felt sticky. He wanted to wash them.

He started forward to the tiny men's lavatory.

Again, from his movements you could get a story of rare physical power compacted in an average-sized frame. This man was just old enough to have a veteran fighter's experience; just young enough to have the fire and endurance of youth. He blended both into a fusion of strength and swiftness that is seldom witnessed.

Alicia Benson smiled at him, and he smiled back with

his vital gray eyes as he opened the door. Little Alice waved a chubby, pink hand at him. He went in.

His hands were not particularly dirty; but one of the characteristics of Richard Benson was a mania for cleanliness. In jungle and arctic wilds, in city and plain, during the amassing of his adventurer's millions, he had carried that craving, washing sometimes when a sip of water was a precious thing.

He laved his hands leisurely and thoroughly and came back into the belly of the plane.

Two seats besides his own were vacant.

The seats occupied by Alicia and little Alice.

Benson stared at the seats with a little prickle of fear at his scalp. But of course everything was all right. The two were only in the rear, in the ladies' lavatory.

The man with the unlit cigar stared at him, then turned stolidly to a window. The other five men and the woman didn't look at him at all. The stewardess came toward him from the rear. Benson beckoned to her.

"Is my wife all right? She's not back there sick, is she?"

"Your wife?" said the stewardess, frowning a little.

"Yes. She isn't ill from the plane motion, is she? Or the little girl?"

"I don't understand," said the stewardess, beginning to look at him very oddly indeed.

Benson's gray eyes flamed through her. The crawling feeling at the nape of his neck grew stronger.

"My wife and daughter," he said distinctly. "The woman and the little girl who were sitting in those two seats in front of mine."

"Those two seats were vacant," said the stewardess.

A little glitter of moisture showed on Benson's forehead. And a glitter like that of steel showed in his pale-gray eyes.

"I simply don't know what you're talking about," the stewardess said. "You didn't get aboard with anyone. You got on alone."

"Are you mad?" snapped Benson. He whirled to the passenger nearest him, the big, flabby man.

"You saw the woman and girl, of course. Tell this pretty fool of a stewardess—"

The flabby man shook his head slowly.

"You're the one who's nuts, brother. You got on alone at Buffalo, like the girl said."

Benson had trusted his life to his almost superhuman hearing in many a wilderness. But he couldn't believe his hearing was correct now. He turned to the others.

"You—all of you! You saw my wife and daughter—"

On all faces he saw the same blank amazement, the same frowns of bewilderment and fear. They were looking at him as if he were crazy.

Benson leaped to the rear of the plane. He slammed open the ladies' lavatory. The small cubicle was empty. He looked into the tail compartment. Only luggage was there, and mail sacks. He jumped to the front of the plane and wrenched open the door to the pilot's compartment. The pilot and copilot stared around at him angrily, then perplexedly as they saw the mounting mania in his pale eyes.

Alicia Benson and little Alice were not aboard the plane.

Benson's voice sounded like strong metal breaking. "Damn you all!" he cried. "What have you done? *Where are they?*"

He went to the door. It was still locked and anyway, with the air pressure outside it would have been practically impossible to open it in flight. He whirled again.

The big, flabby man and the stout fellow with the unlit cigar were moving toward him.

"He's insane," faltered the stewardess. "Get him—"

"No, you don't!" Benson jerked out, in that voice that he himself could hardly recognize. "I'll kill the first man who—"

They retreated a step or two. The other four men got up. Benson's hand went to his hip. He always carried a gun.

"Please," said the stewardess, as one might talk to a child. "You got on alone. You rode alone. There was no one with you. You are having delusions."

"You think I don't know whether or not my wife and daughter were with me?"

Benson went to Alicia's seat.

"The cushion will still be warm. You'll see—"

He put his hand to the cushion. It was cool, as if no one had ever sat in it.

His wife and child were not in the plane. There was no evidence that they ever had been. All the passengers and crew swore they hadn't been. And there was no way for them to have gotten out or been put out.

The pilot's door opened behind him. He had forgotten about that. It opened slowly and without sound the co-pilot hurled a fire extinguisher. It hit the head of the "madman" at whom all were staring in fear.

And Benson went down.

CHAPTER II

Tragedy's Aftermath

Four police and three field attendants—all big, husky men—stayed close to Benson at the Montreal airport. They stayed close because twice they'd had to combine to hold him down when his eyes flamed pale madness and his muscles writhed. His face was chalk-white.

"Phone Buffalo!" Benson said. "I told you—"

"We have phoned," said the airport manager gently. "They have no record of your passage at all."

"I told you we forced our way aboard at the last minute. Of course they haven't a record. But the field men—"

"They all say the same thing. You got aboard alone. You had no wife and daughter."

The police looked at each other significantly.

"My wife! Alice! Where are they? What has happened—Someone believe me! I swear—"

Unbelieving eyes staring down at him! Hand reaching to hold him! Raw electric light battering into his eyes! And at the back of his mind—the lovely face of Alicia and the pink, chubby hand of little Alice upraised to wave—

Something snapped in his head.

An ambulance took him away. But in it was one more interne than the usual pair, and the three of them were extra strong. And they took him, not to a regular hospital, but to a sanitarium—

"Nurse—"

The voice was hoarse, weak. Benson hardly realized

15

it was his own. A girl in white turned from the window of the white-walled room. Benson saw that the window was barred.

"Yes?"

"What time is it?"

"Four thirty in the afternoon," said the nurse, with a professional smile. Benson noted, though, that in her eyes was a look far, indeed, from smiling.

"Half past four! Then I've been out for eighteen or twenty hours!"

"You've been out for three weeks," corrected the nurse. "You've had brain fever."

"Three weeks—"

Benson struggled upright in the bed. "I've got to get out of here! I've got to look for—"

The nurse pushed him firmly back. And finally he let her. He was too weak to do much, and knew it. He was silent for a moment, watching her.

"Why do you look at me like that?" he said. There was in his tired brain a sort of merciful numbness for the moment. It made dreamy and impossible the tragedy that had sent him here. Wife and child vanished apparently into thin air? Nonsense! They'd come in the door at any moment.

"Why do I look at you like that?" repeated the nurse. She hesitated, then shrugged. "You'll have to know eventually. You might as well know now. You've changed, since they carried you in here."

She handed him a mirror. Benson looked into it— and saw somebody else, not himself.

This somebody else had snow-white hair instead of coal-black hair. This somebody had a face as white as linen, instead of a face bronzed by sun and tinted by flowing vitality. This somebody's face, moreover, was as absolutely expressionlesss as a wax mask.

There was something terrible about the expressionlessness. It wasn't normal. It was that of something dead, not that of something living and merely in repose. It frightened you, that completely moveless face.

Benson, with a suffocating feeling rising within him, tried to smile. He couldn't.

Lips, eyebrows all the flesh of his face remained entirely still.

He tried to frown, to grimace—and couldn't.

"The facial muscles are . . . paralyzed," the nurse said gently. "Oh, it's not permanent, probably." Her tone showed that she was lying, to help him. "Probably it will go away. But for now, it's paralyzed. We don't know whether it was the blow on the head you got in the plane when the copilot had to down you, or the nerve shock of your—delusion."

Benson could only stare at the immobile face, that was white as linen, with the pale-gray eyes flaming through. The nurse went back to the window, which she had been closing when he first called her. Benson pressed at his face. He could barely feel the press of his fingers. The nurse turned.

She screamed, then stifled it with her hand.

Benson looked at her, then into the mirror again. And he saw why she had screamed.

He had pressed at his face with his fingers. Where he had pressed, the flesh was ridged up over one cheekbone. It gave him a demoniac look that was indescribable, when added to the linen-pallor of his skin.

He pressed the flesh down again. Then worked both cheeks.

He could move his facial flesh only with his fingers. And wherever he moved it—it stayed!

"I . . . I'm sorry I cried out," faltered the nurse. "But you looked so . . . so *awful*—"

A staff doctor came in.

"Ah! Conscious, eh? And how do we feel?"

Benson's mind was as fast as his body. He'd been conscious only for a few minutes, and after a brain bout that had nearly cost his life. But in that short time he had realized two things.

He must gain strength as rapidly as possible and get out of here.

To get out, he must conceal his colossal agony at the fate of Alicia and little Alice, and indeed pretend as if they had never existed at all.

"I feel much better," he said.

"Fine," said the doctor. "Now as to the matter you were speaking of when we brought you—"

"That is all past," said Benson firmly. He felt a knife turn in his heart—felt as if he were betraying the two who meant all of life to him. But it had to be done.

The doctor's face cleared. "Good man!" he said in a different tone. "I knew you'd get over your delusion. We can have you out of here shortly, I think."

In the doctor's face, Benson saw what he had narrowly missed—detention in the violent ward, maniacs screaming all around him, a padded cell, perhaps. But he had missed it.

In the days that followed, he flexed his muscles and breathed deeply and ate all the rich broths and food they brought. He was storing up strength. And he thought, during the slow hours, tried vainly to figure it out.

What in Heaven's name had happened to Alicia and little Alice? There had been no way for them to get out of that plane. Yet—they'd disappeared from it.

And *why?*

During the days when he built strength back and fought to keep from really going insane with anguish, he asked that question a lot.

Why?

In what horrible criminal plot had he unwittingly thrust his family and himself when he shoved his way aboard that plane? He could not guess. But he knew it must be something gigantic; knew it must be something fiendish. And if he had suffered such an awful loss, there must be others threatened with the same. How many? There was no guessing.

18

He was discharged from the sanitarium. He had gone into the place a man. He came out a machine; a machine of ice and slow fire; a powerful engine geared to only two things—recovery of wife and child and destruction of the force that had acted so fantastically against them.

Benson even looked more like a thing of steel than a man.

Snow-white, his hair was, like chromium. His face, terrible in its utter lack of expression, was steely-white. His eyes, so colorless in his colorless face that you seemed to be looking far, far through them at a chill world of fog and ice, were like pale steel. Even the suit he'd worn in there carried the impression out. It was steely-gray.

At the Montreal airport, he staggered and almost collapsed as he saw a big plane with props idling on the runway. His eyes were dreadful in his white, still face. He knew he could never again look at a plane without feeling that terrific shock. But he also knew that he was going to have to use them—for fast moves of vengeance in the program to which he was dedicating himself.

The agent shrank back a little from the steely-gray figure, moistened his lips at the chill glare of the pale-gray eyes.

"Y-yes, sir," he stammered. "There's a seat in the Buffalo plane."

"Thank you," said Benson. His lips barely moved with the words. They seemed to come, of their own volition, from great, white, still spaces back of those pale and flaming eyes.

He went to the plane. Attendants made way for him and stared after him. But he paid no attention. Alone in the glacial, terrible world of his grief, he boarded the plane and roared back along the track of tragedy.

CHAPTER III

The First Clue

Never had a man chanced to be in less of a position to prove that he'd ever had a wife and daughter than Dick Benson.

For two years, since he had acquired his last half million in an Australian amethyst venture, he and his young wife and little Alice had played over a large part of the globe. Bermuda Hawaii, California, Florida, Alaska—all had seen them. In Buffalo they'd stayed at a hotel for a few days. They had no locality, no neighbors—they'd been rich vagabonds.

But Benson had to get some place or person to prove his story so he could get the aid of the police.

He went to the hotel. The assistant manager said of course he'd met Mrs. Benson and the daughter. That was before they'd gone to Louisiana.

"What are you talking about?" snapped Benson.

The man flinched at the glare in the pale eyes.

"The clerk said that's where they went."

Benson went to the clerk who'd been on duty when they checked out.

Yes, he'd seen Mr. Benson go out with Mrs. Benson and the child. Then he'd gotten the forwarding letter.

"What letter?" said Benson, lips barely moving in his dead, white face.

"The letter Mrs. Benson wrote saying she was going to New Orleans and to forward mail to the Picayune Hotel there."

"She went with me to Montreal."

"Of course, sir, if you say so," the clerk muttered.

Benson got hold of the cab driver who had taken them to the field.

"Yes, sir, you got in at the hotel with a lady and a little girl. I drove you to the airline ticket office downtown. You all got out there. The lady and the little girl didn't get back into the cab with you. They stayed downtown."

Benson's hand, went out like a darting snake. He got the driver by the collar and those steely-slim fingers of his showed what just a little pressure would do.

"Please! You're choking—" The driver stared into the appalling gray eyes with his own like those of a frightened rabbit. "I *swear* you went to the airport alone! I'd . . . I'd swear it in court!"

Benson marked him down for the future, and went to the Buffalo airport. Behind came a dark green sedan with three men in it, but he didn't see that. He stared straight ahead, a gray steel bar of a man with pale and awful eyes staring into a future that held but one hope— finding again all that made life worth living for him.

At the airport, the agent moistened his lips as Dick Benson approached, moving on the balls of his feet, eyes alert and sinister as a jaguar's.

"You remember me?" said Benson, lips hardly moving in his paralyzed, linen-white face.

The agent gulped. "Yes, sir," he said, staring hard.

"I came in here with my wife and little girl, a month ago, to get places for Montreal."

The agent was shivering as if with palsy. But he shook his head.

"I don't remember that. I only remember you. You came in alone. There was a phone call about that from Montreal, later. And I said the same thing. You were alone—"

His voice trailed off. His face was literally green, but there was no shaking his story.

Again Benson realized what a terrible force there must be behind this. This man *knew* better. He *had* remembered the brown-eyed Alicia and the girl, Alice. His eyes showed it. But something—*something*—had him so frightened that even with Benson's pale and flaming eyes on him, he lied. And the cab driver had lied.

Benson went out to the field, leaving the agent white and cowering in the office. Again, he stared, straight ahead, with visions of his wife and child filling his world. So he did not notice the three men from the dark sedan who went furtively into the office after he'd gone.

"O.K., pal," one said to the shivering agent. "You know what happens to squealers."

"I didn't squeal!" the agent sobbed. "I didn't say a word. I swore he'd come in alone. That *face* of his!"

The man in the lead thrust a gun against the agent's belly.

"Which scares you most, pal, his face or this?"

But the reaction was not quite what the gunman had bargained for.

"I don't know," the man shivered. "The face . . . is almost as bad . . . as a gun!"

Outside, Benson went to the nearest hangar. A group of men there watched him approach. They stared curiously at the dead face, looked uneasily at the flaming ice of Benson's eyes.

He stared at them collectively, and each man flinched a little when the cold gaze struck him.

"A month ago," he said, lips curiously immobile in his paralyzed face, "I took a plane from this field for Montreal. I got aboard with my wife and small daughter. Do any of you remember?"

Slowly, they all shook their heads. Benson felt as if he were fighting fog, pillows, and substance that made no resistance to his hardest blows—and yet barred him like a stone wall. However, it was possible that these men, at least, were telling the truth. He didn't remember seeing any of them that day.

Out on the field near the broad runway he saw a

bony, knobby figure of a man with ears that stuck out like sails on each side of a thick-skinned red neck.

He remembered that man and hurried toward him through a red fog of torment.

"You," he said, to the field attendant who had put him and his family aboard that day. For a moment he could not go on. This was his last chance. If *this* man lied—

The man moved slowly off, away from the hangars—and from his white-faced questioner. Benson went after him. The last notch of his iron will had been reached. He was ready to tear this tall, bony figure apart. He was ready to rend and slash—

"Easy, mon," the attendant said out of the corner of his mouth. "I know what ye'd be asking me, and I'm moving from the hangars so nobody can hear. We can't talk here. The field itself has ears. What hotel are ye stopping at?"

Benson told him. "You . . . you—"

"I'll have something to tell ye, soon as I can get away from here."

Benson literally staggered. A crack in this dreadful blackness at last!

"Hotel Ely," he said. "Come fast, for the love of God!"

He went to the gate. He didn't see the three men there, either. They drew a little closer. One got out a gun, but a second caught his arm. The second stared meaningly around at the airport, with frequent figures on it, and shook his head. This was no plcae to use a gun, his gesture said.

Benson got into his cab, blind with relief, and started off toward the Hotel Ely. He had his man, now. There was something honest in that Scotchman's narrow, bitter face, with its stony blue eyes. He'd talk. Benson could go to the police now—

But even as he thought that, he knew he couldn't. It was this one man's word against a dozen others. No police force would believe so bizarre a tale, on that lopsided witnessing, that a man's wife and daughter could disappear from a speeding airliner.

No, he'd have to go it alone. He knew that. And his steely body yearned savagely for the fight, while his mind raced on ahead to the slight hope that he'd get Alicia and little Alice back—

A green sedan shot past the cab, angled in, and the cab driver applied his brakes with a squeal of tortured rubber. Benson stared out.

He saw that the cab was in a deserted spot, on the outskirts of Buffalo, in a marsh flat with distant factories bounding it.

The sedan had deliberately forced the cab to the roadside. Benson saw that in a flash, and reached for his gun. But he had no gun. It had been taken from him at the Montreal sanitarium.

"Ram that car!" he snapped to the driver.

The man, wild with fear, either didn't hear or didn't obey. The cab slowed still more.

Benson reached through the front window, curled his hand around the man's throat and jerked back. The driver's foot slipped from the brake. The cab bounded forward.

In the sedan, two of the three men had guns out and windows rolled down. The driver saw the cab careen toward them as the brakes were released. He swerved wide to avoid it. The two men swerved wide to avoid it. The two men with the gun were jerked sideways so that their shots went wild.

The cab hit the sedan with a grinding roar.

Benson was out of it almost before the noise had died away, and was leaping for the sedan. Not away from it, and its guns, but toward it. In his pale-gray eyes there was a savage, icy smile at the prospect of at last coming to grips with something solid.

That cold and awful smile in the gray flame of his eyes was later to become a hallmark of Dick Benson. With death closing in on him, with the odds hopelessly

25

against him, the smile would appear in the gray ice of his eyes, as though he welcomed death, or at least did not care a snap of his fingers if it struck.

The sedan had rocked away from the cab, almost tipped, then rocked back again on four wheels. And while the three men inside were still fighting for their balance, Benson had the rear door open and was in it.

Just an average-sized man—Richard Henry Benson. Five feet eight, certainly no more than a hundred and sixty pounds. Not at all a big man.

But there is quality as well as quantity to muscle. Ounce for ounce, some muscle tissue is twice as powerful as the ordinary. Now and then you get a man like Benson in whom, ounce for ounce, sinew and muscle are packed with force beyond any scientific explanation. And these rare men do things that are incredible to the average mortal.

With his left hand still on the door lock of the green sedan, Benson's right lashed out. There was less than a ten-inch swing behind it. But his fist hit the jaw of the nearest man like a knob of iron on the end of an iron lance. The man fell back against his pal as if he had been shot.

Benson caught the wrist of the driver, who was hastily poking a gun over the back of the front seat at him. The gun exploded, but tore a harmless hole in the top of the sedan. One-handed, Benson twisted the arm he held. The driver moaned, then screamed and slumped in the seat.

Eyes like holes in glacier ice, Benson returned to the third man, who was clawing to get out from under the hampering bulk of his unconscious partner.

Unable to get his gun in line, the man kicked frantically at Benson's head. And that was a mistake.

The slim and terrible right hand went out. The steely-white fingers caught the calf of the vicious leg. And Benson squeezed. That was all, just squeezed.

The man yelled out and dropped his gun. Up his body,

from vital nerve points streamed pain too great to be borne. He yelled again and, yelling, dropped. He did not move when Benson took his hand away.

The cab driver came timorously closer. It was very still, there on the deserted section of road. Had anyone been around to hold a stop watch on the proceedings, he would have found that less than ten seconds had elapsed from the time Benson got the sedan door open to the time when the third man dropped senseless from the deft and awful pressure on the great nerves of his leg.

"Gee!" whispered the cab driver. He seemed to search for other words, staring, meanwhile, at the dead, white face of the man who had done these things—a face all the more awe-inspiring in that even at this crowded moment, not one line of it altered in the least. "Gee!"

Benson took the three to the Buffalo police station. Then he went to his hotel.

And in less than half an hour he got a phone call.

The three men had been sprung.

Someone—who, no one at headquarters knew—had sent one of Buffalo's best lawyers to get writs of habeas corpus. Someone had put up cash bail as if thousands were small change.

And the three gunmen were free.

Benson hung up with pale-gray eyes like ice in a glacial dawn. Not the fault of the police. Some power too big even for them was behind all this. But he wouldn't make this mistake again.

Because the police are sometimes hampered more than helped by law, those three had been turned loose. And Benson knew that he'd probably never see them again.

CHAPTER IV

Benson's Ally

His name was Fergus MacMurdie. He was over six feet, and had coarse red hair and bitter blue eyes and hands that doubled into fists like bone clubs. His feet were the biggest Benson had ever seen, and they made the bony legs above them look even bonier.

The man from the airport had come, and stood now before him with his hat in his raw, red left hand. In the last few days Benson had become accustomed to the sight of men viewing his white and terrible face with a trace of fear in their eyes. But this man did not. He didn't look as if he'd ever be afraid of anything. With the deep lines of his freckle-splotched face, and the grim, stony look of his intensely blue eyes, he gave the impression of a man who had had all fear burned from him in some travail of the soul.

"MacMurdie," Benson said, "you saw me get aboard the plane with my wife and little girl?"

"Of course, mon," said MacMurdie.

"They stayed aboard with me? They didn't get off before we left?"

"Sure, they stayed aboard with ye."

Benson looked at the Scot's mallet-like right hand. There was skin missing from the knuckles. At the edge of the Scotchman's sandy hair line the blue of a bruise showed.

"What happened?" said Benson.

MacMurdie's bitter blue eyes narrowed.

"Some at the airfield guessed I'd said something to ye, I'm thinkin'. Anyhow, outside, two men jumped me. I left 'em there."

Benson's set, white face remained as still as a thing in death. But his eyes were puzzled.

"Power behind this," he said, lips barely moving. "Money. Many men. People bribed, the forces of the law overcome—just to prove to the world that I got on the plane alone—that I never had a wife and daughter. You know that's what they tell me, don't you, MacMurdie?"

"I know," said the dour Scot.

The pale-gray eyes played coldly over his face.

"Why didn't you turn your two attackers over to the police, MacMurdie?"

"I've done wi' the police," the Scot said grimly.

"You mean—a jail sentence in your past?"

"No. 'Tis not because of that. The police are all right, as far as they go, but they don't go far enough. At least, they didn't wi' me."

The pale-gray eyes expressed the question that the rest of the face could not.

"You see me a field attendant," said MacMurdie, spreading his bony red hands. "Not much more than a laborer. But I wasn't, once. I owned four drugstores. I'm a licensed pharmacist. I attended three years medical school, but I was too poor to finish."

The bitter blue eyes matched the cold gray ones, flame for flame.

"I had a wife, too. I had a boy. And men came round and said to me, 'MacMurdie,' they said, 'your stores are likely to be bombed some night if you don't take out a memberhip in our protective association, which costs two hundred dollars a month for four fine stores like yours.' So I told 'em where they could go, and I told 'em twice. And then—"

The knobby, huge hands clenched and quivered.

"My biggest store *was* bombed. It was at six at night. Mrs. MacMurdie was there and so was my boy."

The look in Benson's ice-gray eyes was gentler than it had been since the terrible plane ride.

"The police did what they could," MacMurdie went on. "I'll say that for 'em. But nobody seemed to do anything. No one but the undertaker. I let the stores slide. Since then I've drifted. When I get the chance, I smash the crooked skurlies like the two that jumped me outside the airport. But call in the police? What for? It'd do me no good now, or ever again."

Benson stared into the stony-blue eyes for a long time. He was a judge of men, and he could see no deceit in this man's dim-freckled face.

"It seems we've both lost all a man has to lose, MacMurdie. And it seems we're both beyond the power even of the police to help. But maybe we can help each other. Will you help me in this?"

"Gladly, if I can," said the Scot.

"Then tell me, have you any idea what's behind this? Why were my wife and little girl spirited away? What plan did I interrupt when I got aboard that plane? Who hired the men who attacked you, and three more who also attacked me a while before that?"

MacMurdie shook his sandy-red head.

"I'd tell ye, mon, if I could. But I don't know the answers to any of those questions."

"Then you know nothing at all?"

"Whoosh! I wasn't sayin' that. I know a few things that I've thought about more than once. One is that about that same crowd has booked the Buffalo-Montreal plane solid four times in the last three weeks. Another is that always every seat is bought—but two or three are always empty when the plane goes up. A third is that always there's a trunk goes aboard, though 'tis seldom folks travel in planes wi' trunks. What is it, mon?"

Benson had gotten up from his chair with one tigerish surge of muscle. He was glaring at the Scot, with his eyes like gray holes in his white, dead face.

"A trunk! I saw one in the tail when I searched for

my wife! She—they—could have been hidden and taken off at Montreal in that—"

Then, slowly, he sat down again. He had remembered something more.

He had seen that trunk, and it had been open, with the lid thrown back—and empty. This hope, at least, of sometimes seeing Alicia and little Alice again, was futile.

"Maybe they're dead," he whispered. "I'm afraid they are dead. If not—I'll find them. If they are—I'll make that gang of crooks, whoever they are, wish they'd never been born!"

"And how are ye fixin' to do that?" said MacMurdie. "You, one man alone, against a whole gang, and them with big money and big power behind them?"

"I'll do it!" said Benson.

MacMurdie's bitter blue eyes traveled over Benson. Of only average height and weight, not looking exceptionally powerful. Only the deadly pale eyes in the dead white face compelled attention.

MacMurdie was a practical man.

"What have ye got to fight with, Muster Benson?"

"I have a great deal of money, though few except the income-tax department know it."

"Ye'll have to have more than that."

"I made the money," said Benson, "in wild countries, and with men who make city gangsters look meek. I've located mines in the arctic. I've taken emeralds from Brazil. I brought a forty-thousand-dollar cargo of animals to the Cleveland Zoo from the Malay jungles. I held a crew in mutiny across the Pacific for twenty-three days. I don't talk of these things much, but you asked me what I had to fight with."

"You're not so big," said MacMurdie doubtfully.

Benson got up and went to him.

"Hit me," he said.

"Whoosh! I'm twice as big as ye!"

"Hit me. As hard as you can."

The Scot could use his hands. He feinted cleverly

32

with his left for Benson's abdomen, then sizzled a right to Benson's jaw that would have knocked him out.

And Benson swayed two inches, caught the flying knobby fist and bore down. The Scot turned almost a complete somersault and banged to the floor.

"Ye'll do," he said, getting up and blinking bewilderedly at the man with the set, still face.

"I have still another little weapon," said Benson. "I seem to have acquired it with the shock of this thing."

He turned from the Scot. There was a mirror over the dresser near the window. Benson looked into that, moving his hands over his face. Then he turned.

MacMurdie visibly started, then slowly whistled.

When Benson had turned from him his face was his own, well-cast and regular-featured though, of course, devoid of all expression. When he turned back, the transformation was startling. High cheekbones gave Benson a Chinese expression. The corners of the immobile mouth were turned down in a sinister fashion. The ears set forward a little. Even the forehead was altered, pressed into a narrower line with deep wrinkles where the smooth skin had been.

It was the face of another man.

"I wouldn't know ye," said MacMurdie, voice awed, "if it weren't for the white hair."

"I can wear a hat to cover that," said Benson. "With a few outside aids, I think I can disguise more quickly and perfectly than any other man in the world today. And *that* won't hurt any in our war on these murderers."

He rearranged his face into its normal lines, flesh staying plastically in whatever outline his deft fingers prodded it.

"We've got to get a starting point for our investigations, MacMurdie."

The Scot nodded slowly. "Yes, an' I think we may have one, Muster Benson. 'Tis one more thing I thought of, and was going to tell ye when ye shocked me out of a year's sleep by changing your face like that. Ye say

33

your wife and little girl simply vanished from that plane?"

"Yes," said Benson. His pale eyes were stricken at the mention of Alicia and little Alice, but his face was a mask. "They . . . just vanished. Though that's impossible. The regular door can scarcely be opened on a plane in flight. There's no other way for them to have gotten out. But . . . they disappeared!"

"Well, here's somethin' that may help ye," MacMurdie said. "The Great Lakes Airline, owners of the plane ye took to Montreal, have bought some of their crates secondhand. One of 'em they picked up from the United States Coast Survey. It was a plane they used to make maps with."

Instantly the flashing brain behind the pale-gray eyes got it. Comprehension glittered in their gray-ice depths.

"That same plane," MacMurdie went on, "was used last year. 'Twas in all the papers. The airline sent it up to Hudson Bay with their best pilot—and they dropped food and supplies to a bunch of starving miners blizzard-bound two hundred miles from civilization."

Once more Benson was on his feet, rising in the single surge of lithe, tigerish power.

"A trapdoor!" he snapped. "By all that's holy—of course! A trapdoor!"

"An' there," nodded MacMurdie, "may be our startin' point. Though a startin' point to nothing but a slug in the pump for each of us, I'm thinkin'. We can't win in a game like this. We're bound to be flattened out."

Later, Benson was to learn that the dour Scot was always a predicter of disaster. Nothing could possibly succeed; nothing gave the man any hope—until he was actually into battle. Then, and then only, did a sort of hard grin appear on his somber lips. Then, and then only, did he predict sure success where any other man on earth would have been convinced of failure.

"Then we'll be flattened out," said Benson shortly. "But we'll flatten a few others first. What was the number of the plane I rode in, MacMurdie?"

"The S404. That's the one with the door in its belly."

"I'll have a look at it," said Benson. He began to write on a sheet of hotel stationery. "But on my way to the airport, I'll make a few stops. Meanwhile, you take this note to an old, old friend of mine. On reading it, the friend will give you two things—something I thought I'd never have to use again, something I meant to keep out of my life since I retired with a fortune from adventurous money-making. You bring them back here. I'll probably be back as soon as you are."

"Right," nodded MacMurdie. Then he looked curiously at the dead, white face that, no matter what the situation or emotional strain, could never express a sentiment.

"What stops do ye make on your way to the airport, Muster Benson?"

"I'm stopping at the best tailoring establishment in town. Also at a theatrical costumer's. Also at a rubber-goods novelty shop. Be careful with those two things you get from my old friend, MacMurdie. It would be very hard to duplicate either of them."

CHAPTER V

The Camouflaged Plane

The agent at the Buffalo airport looked curiously at the man across the counter from him. He had a vague feeling that he'd seen the man before, somewhere—and yet he knew that he could not have.

The man was of average height, but seemed short because his shoulders were so broad and he was so stocky. He wore a flat-brimmed hat with a slightly Western look. His face was flat and broad, with deep, weather-bitten lines. He moved slowly, and looked almost sleepy, with his narrowed, expressionless eyes.

The eyes were very light gray, almost colorless.

"We don't usually charter planes for so long, or to go such distances, Mr. Conroy," the agent said. "You want it for work in Nevada, you say? Why don't you get a plane from a Western company?"

"I told you," said the man. "This work is to be kept secret. I'd rather have a pilot from two thousand miles away than do business with a local firm."

He shifted slightly bowed legs under him as though lonesome for the feel of a horse on the open range.

"Like I said, I'm a prospector. I located this claim in a place where only prospectors and mountain goats can go. No chance of getting in machinery by burro. So I want a plane to drop a little light machinery by parachute. And I understand you have a plane with a trapdoor, which would be just the ticket."

The agent hesitated quite a long time. Then he said:

"I'm afraid your information is incorrect. We have no planes with trapdoors."

The man's narrowed gray eyes expressed disappointment. His face remained dead-pan, expressed nothing at all.

"Oh. I understood you had such a plane. I'm sorry I bothered you. I'll have to go somewhere else."

He nodded and left the office.

It was dark, by now. Late dusk. Lights flooded the field, of course; but his figure could only dimly be seen as he went to the gate and the cab there. He got into the cab.

The broad shoulders were caused by rubber pads, that could be inflated, over the shoulder caps. Benson deflated them. The Western-looking hat held that shape because in brim and crown fine wire was laced in the felt, unseen.

Benson altered the hat till it was Homburg style. He prodded his face. It had been broad and rather flat, deeply lined. It now became subtly leaner, smooth and extra full around the lips. He slipped his spring topcoat off and put it on inside out. It had been gray, checked. Now it was solid brown with a narrow, formal velvet collar.

It had only taken thirty seconds to make the change, but that was enough for the cab driver, sitting stolidly in front and waiting for orders, to get impatient.

"Where to, boss?" he said over his shoulder, not bothering to look around.

"Ely Hotel," said Benson.

And he slipped out the side of the cab opposite the airport gate. The cab drove off, empty. Benson went back into the field.

He was slim, dapper, younger-looking than his years. He no more resembled the "prospector from Nevada" than Jack Dempsey resembles Tom Thumb.

He went directly to the biggest hangar, in which the large airliners were kept. He walked with that curious air of authority which some men can acquire, and which causes people instinctively to let them pass even though sometimes ordinary mortals are not allowed to. Several mechanics and field men stared at him as he entered the hangar, but after a hesitation, did not offer to bar his way.

In the huge shed were two liners. One had the figures H61 on its bulging nose. And the other was numbered— S402.

S402! It was S404 that MacMurdie said that had the opening in the bottom. Benson stared at the figures with eyes that glittered disappointment, even though his face never moved in line.

Then those quick, pale eyes of his, trained in a hundred deadly ventures to see things normal eyes did not observe, noticed something.

The gray paint on the airliner's fuselage was well-kept but not new.

The paint of the figures themselves *did* seem new.

The nose loomed far above him. But, standing under it and staring up with eyes like a hawk's in their telescopic-microscopic powers, he made sure of it. The figures had been painted on that ship later than the fuselage. Quite recently, in fact.

"So they've prepared for investigation," Benson whispered.

Someone might look at the ship in which two souls had fantastically and impossibly vanished. So somebody had switched numbers. It was the S404 that he had traveled in. It was the S404 that had the trapdoor. But this ship was numbered S402.

Benson moved to the side. He climbed up into the fuselage. Into the body of the big plane. Light from the hangar penetrated the airliner's windows and gave him dim illumination.

There was a thick carpet on the floor. It seemed to run under the seats, but as he tugged at it a strip rose in his hands. He folded it back. And there, in the metal floor was an oblong crack six by three.

39

The trapdoor.

Benson was a strong man, to begin with. And he had been tempered in the fire of an almost unendurable tragedy till he was hardly a man; he was a machine of vengeance. But the sight of this thing brought back in a rush all the awful torture of his loss.

Through that oblong, gravelike in its dimensions, his Alicia and their wee Alice had been dropped. There was no doubt of it. It was the only thing to explain the bizarre disappearance.

Far over the grim black surface of Lake Ontario, those two he loved had been dropped. Slugged first, perhaps, to prevent outcry! Who knew? Equipped hurriedly with parachutes, just possibly, so they'd land alive? He tried fiercely to believe that—and could not. The only motive for such a thing would have been a kidnap plot against them. And he had received no ransom demand since the terrible trip.

Benson leaned forward. His forehead touched the back of one of the seats and rested there. His shoulders shook a little in the last extremity of torment.

And all the time—his face did not move a muscle. Not a line! It was a dreadful thing to see that dead face so changeless in spite of the raging tornado behind it.

Through that opening, into the black water thousands of feet below—

It was while he leaned shuddering there, for the moment as helpless as a child in his colossal grief, that the dark figure crept into the plane behind him from the hangar.

Ordinarily a thousand little nerves would have felt the tiny shift of the plane on its great landing wheels as a man's weight was added to it. Ordinarily a sense of hearing miraculously keen would have caught the faint rasp of moving clothes. But coming up behind the steel-spring adventurer with the deadly cold eyes just now was as easy as approaching a blind man.

The figure behind Benson paused a moment. Then its

40

arm went up. Light glittered on a heavy wrench. The arm came down—

At the Hotel Ely, MacMurdie waited in the lobby. He had gone to the address of the friend given him by Benson. Under his arm was a small but heavy package. MacMurdie did not know what was in the package. He was waiting for Benson to come and take it, and tell, if he pleased, what he'd found out at the flying field.

But Benson did not come. And MacMurdie's dour blue eyes went more coldly blue than ever.

Something in the man with the dead, white face from which the pale eyes peered so icily, had got under the skin of the lonely Scot. He was as worried by Benson's continued absence as he would be if he'd known the man for ten years instead of as many hours.

There was a commotion at the desk. MacMurdie looked in that direction. A taxicab driver was arguing with the clerk.

"—looked back into the rear, and the guy wasn't there. All the way to the airport and back on the meter. I want my dough."

MacMurdie got up and walked toward the desk. The clerk said something he couldn't hear.

"He's said to come here to the Hotel Ely. He must be registered here. Naw, I don't know his name. But I want my dough for that trip to the airport and back."

MacMurdie's knobby, malletlike hand came down on the driver's shoulder.

"Who are ye talking about, mon?"

"Some guy, looked like he was from the West. Picked me up outside a tailor shop downtown here. Had me take him to the airport. Then he took a run-out powder somewhere between the gate and here. And I'm stuck for the fare."

"What did he look like?"

"I don't remember much, except his eyes. They were very light gray."

MacMurdie's bony hand tightened till the driver yelped, then loosened.

"Wha' is the bill?"

"Four dollars and ten cents."

MacMurdie got out an ancient leather purse, with a clip snap. He opened it, took out four one-dollar bills, a nickel and five pennies.

He counted it carefully into the man's hands.

"You throw your dough around in tips, don't you?" said the driver sarcastically.

"Only a fool is prodigal wi' his money," said the Scot. "And now ye can take *me* out to that airport, as fast as you can navigate."

He handed the small, heavy package to the clerk.

"Keep this till Muster Benson and me return."

He felt like adding dourly, "If we *do* return." But he didn't.

He entered the airport gate from the cab with his hat pulled down low. He had been fired from here. They'd not let him in if they saw him.

He got past the office all right, and out to the hangar. They were wheeling out one of the big ships. S402 was painted on her nose. One of the mechanics waved to the Scot. They'd all liked him when he worked here. But another of the men, a fellow with dark hair growing down on his forehead and mean dark eyes set too close together, backed out of MacMurdie's sight and then began running toward the airport administration building.

MacMurdie went up to the plane. The man who had waved, grinned at him.

"So they bounced you, Mac?" he said. "What was wrong? Drunk again?"

"I don't touch the spirit of the vine, as well ye know, Tommy," MacMurdie said. " 'Twas a personal disagreement. Is this the S402? And how did it get the duralumin patch in the wing, and Dunlop-tread tires on the landin' wheels, like the S404?"

"Why, now that you mention it," said Tommy, staring, "you're right! That's funny! A guy was painting around here the other day, freshening up the numbers. I wonder if the dope could have got the wrong—Hey, Stock."

Stock was the boss mechanic. MacMurdie waited with muscles tense for the answer to the call. But there wasn't any answer.

"Stock!"

"He ain't here," said another of the men, coming from under the transport's wing. "Guy got sick in the hangar a while ago. Some bird I never saw before. And Stock took him out—to a doctor's, I guess. Anyhow, he ain't back."

MacMurdie was listening as though life depended on catching every last syllable with his big, outstanding ears.

"Guy sick in the hangar? Who?"

"I don't know. I tell you I never saw him before. Somebody in from off the street. He was hanging around this boat, the S402, last I saw him. Then Stock and another guy came out supporting him like he'd keeled over in a faint. Don't know what happened or where they went, but Stock ain't back yet—"

From the office came the agent and two men who kept their hands near their armpits. MacMurdie saw them out of the corners of his somber blue eyes. And MacMurdie left. Fast!

He moved toward the airport gate, and the three moved to intercept him. They got to the gate at about the same time.

"MacMurdie! What the devil are you doing—"

The Scot didn't take time to reply to the agent. He didn't wait for the hands of the other two men to be withdrawn from under their lapels.

The two were little and ratlike. They had only one thing to fight with—guns. And they were handicapped because they couldn't quite make up their minds to use them in the presence of so many airport attendants.

So while they were chewing their lips, the Scot's long, bony arms swept out.

Each hamlike hand got a man's collar. He jerked the two forward, then flung them back, with his huge right foot in the path of their feet. They tripped against the agent. The three went down.

MacMurdie leaped into the cab.

"Away from here, mon! Fast!"

The cab started forward. In a minute MacMurdie would give a definite address. He thought he knew where to go next.

He knew Stock, the boss mechanic, pretty well. Knew him as thoroughly as he disliked him. Stock had a small farm ten miles out of town. A shack of a place. If the "guy who was sick" was Benson, as MacMurdie was sure, and if Stock and others wanted to get rid of him, it was quite likely they'd take him to that secluded, desolate farm.

MacMurdie leaned forward to tell the driver to go out there. But before he could do that, there was action from behind.

One of the ratlike little gunmen had his automatic braced on his forearm, pistol-gallery style. Its sight was square on the hat to be seen in the back window of the cab, now thirty yards away.

The man squeezed the trigger. There was a galvanic movement of the hat, and then it went slowly forward out of sight.

"There!" said the man. "That'll fix 'im! Got him square through the head. That'll learn guys to come poking around here on things that don't concern them!"

CHAPTER VI

Mac Gums The Works

Benson's senses slowly returned to the tune of a swaying, bumping, rapid motion that at first he couldn't recognize. Then he got it. He was in the speeding automobile. He kept his eyes closed because his head hurt so much that he didn't want the shock of light added to them. Then he continued to keep them closed because a voice from just above him sounded out.

"Who do you suppose the rummy is?"

"How would I know?" snarled another voice from a little ahead of him.

But it was the first voice that shocked Benson instantly into full consciousness and threw the mental gears that sent his fast, precise brain instantly into full speed.

He remembered other words, at a world-shaking moment.

"You're nuts, brother. You got on alone at Buffalo."

Those words had been uttered by this voice that night when he'd come out of the men's washroom to find his wife and child gone.

Very slowly, and only a little way, he opened his eyes.

He was jammed down on the floor in the back of a closed car. There was no light on the dash forward, but at intervals light from the street lamps came in the windows. He saw, on the back seat above him, a large, flabby man with a gun in his hand.

It was one of the men who had been on the Buffalo-

Montreal plane—one who had insisted Benson never had a wife and child!

The man glanced down, and Benson quickly closed his eyes again. He was not bound, but the gun was very alert on him. Suicide to try anything now. In a moment it became even more suicidal to think of resistance, because the street lights stopped as the car left town and began rolling along country roads. Now Benson couldn't even see the gun to grab for it.

"I wonder who this sucker is," puzzled the flabby man in the back seat.

"Your guess's good as mine," said the driver.

"I thought for a minute I'd seen the guy before. But if I did, it must have been a long time ago. I don't know any bloke with white hair and a face like that. Mebbe it's some private dick I bumped into years ago."

"Private dick's a good gamble," observed the driver, in his cruel, metallic voice. "Probably some guy hired by that mug, Benson."

His words ended in a string of curses. And Benson digested the situation with his fast, flashing mind.

He had recognized the flabby man from the plane. But the man had not recognized him. The whitening of his hair, and the paralysis of his face, from the shock, had served him well in this case.

"Too bad you guys didn't get Benson, too, there in the plane," said the unseen driver.

Benson listened so hard it hurt. Light on that horrible night? Perhaps.

The flabby man grunted.

"If you'd been there you wouldn't say that. The guy comes out with blood in his eye. See? And he's got a mean eye, anyhow. Light gray. Gives you the creeps to look into 'em. He roars around for a while, lookin' everywhere. And all the time he has a gun. See? Sure, we oughtta got him, too. And we would have. But not with that gun in his mitt. See? By the time Fred could get back from the pilot's compartment and jump him, we're over Montreal. Then we can't drop him out. Somebody might spot us. And we can't circle out to dump him in the open, because that might get somebody suspicious. All we can do is land with him—and make that story of ours stick. And we did, too."

"Yeah. Sure, you did." The driver's voice was ironical. "You made it stick so hard the guy's breakin' his neck to find out what happened!"

"Well, how'd we know he had a lot of dough, and was a tough customer? He was just a sap who got in the way, to us. Like some others we've put *out* of the way before now—and a lot of others we'll probably have to knock off before we're through."

"This is big stuff, ain't it?" said the driver, with a note almost of fright in his voice.

"I'll say it's big! If the cops ever got a gander at it, they'd lay eggs! But there's big guys behind it, so don't go getting scared. We got a million dollars' worth of protection any time we need it."

"What's it about, anyhow?" asked the driver.

All Benson's functioning seemed to be in those acute ears of his. If this question were answered—
But it wasn't.

"I don't know myself," said the flabby man, complainingly. "The big shots don't take us guys into their confidence much. All I know is, Old Ironsides is one of the—"

"Watch it!" snapped the driver. "That stooge detective of Benson's might be awake."

There was silence. Then a toe ground into Benson's ribs. Benson's pale-gray eyes flamed with a deadly anger behind closed lids, but he stayed moveless.

"Out like a light," said the flabby man.

But he didn't say any more. Neither did the driver. The car sped on. No way of telling how far. Benson couldn't check on the speed. Somewhere between ten and twenty miles, the last mile or so of which was over a bumpy dirt road. He judged he had been taken to a

47

very secluded place. And in a moment the car stopped and he saw that he was right.

"Dump him out!"

Benson was hauled out of the car by the legs and allowed to fall on neck and shoulders in the gravel of a lane. Tree toads shrilled and crickets fiddled around him. The night was filled with the noisy silence of the country.

He opened his eyes a little again. He saw the dark bulk of a frame farmhouse, the slanting line of an old barn.

"In the barn," said the flabby man. "Then we'll bury him under the floor. You said there was an old cistern there, didn't you?"

"Yeah."

"Well, we'll throw him in there and put a couple of loads of dirt over him and then nail the floor back. After that this Benson guy can call out the bloodhounds for his investigator—and see how much good it does him."

"You guys don't care how many chances you take on my place, do you?" said the driver bitterly. Benson could see him now. He was a blocky man in the white work coat of a shop foreman. Wings were on the coat. Evidently he was the head mechanic from the airfield.

"We're taking no chances," soothed the flabby man. He leveled his gun.

"Hey! We're a mile from the nearest house. But you got no idea how sound carries out here! Don't use a slug."

"O.K., then," said the flabby man. "Where's a good thick club? We'll knock him on the head like a steer."

"I got better than a club. Wait."

The man in the white work coat disappeared, came back with something in his hand. It was a heavy hatchet, rusted, but with quite a sharp edge.

"Here you go."

The flabby man took the hatchet. His manner was as impersonal as that of an executioner wielding a headsman's ax. The taking of a life was obviously no novelty to him.

He raised the hatchet, grunted a little with the preliminary effort of the blow to be struck, and brought it whistling down.

Benson, with an explosive move as violent and efficient as it was totally unexpected, writhed to one side.

The blade fairly whistled past his ear, missing it by less than an inch. The hatchet buried itself in the ground almost up to the handle. And then Benson had the wrist behind the weapon.

The airfield mechanic was yelling and charging now. Benson pulled the flabby man forward onto his face with one powerful jerk—and jerked himself erect at the same time and with the same move. His fist caught the mechanic's flying body just over the heart, and the man staggered back, moaning.

The flabby man was on his knees with his gun in his hand. Benson's leg came out with the lithe move of a dancer's, multipied by ten in point of power. His toe caught the man's elbow. There was a little snap, and the gun flew thirty feet away while the flabby man grabbed at his arm.

The airport man took a step back to charge again. But he stopped. In the dimness of the night he could still see Benson's face—still and icy-white and with no more expression than if Benson were merely talking about the weather. It was indescribably unnerving, such utter lack of emotion on a face at such a time. And the deadly pale eyes that glared from the moveless white mask were equally unnerving.

The man's ratlike courage melted like sugar in a rain. He cried out almost like a child in fear, turned, and ran from that terrible countenance of vengeance.

The flabby man, broken forearm clutched in his agonized left hand, had already started toward the car. Both were getting away.

Benson jerked the hatchet from the ground. He threw it.

In a long flat arc it flashed after the mechanic. The throw was a beautiful thing. No Indian could have thrown a tomahawk like that. It was all the more perfect in that it missed the man's head in precisely the way Benson intended.

Had the blade edge struck, it would have sliced the running man's skull almost in two. Had the flat edge hit, it would have crushed his head like an eggshell. But it was the handle that struck, at the base of the skull, and knocked the man unconscious for many minutes to come, without actually killing him.

Benson was in motion the instant the hatchet left his steely fingers. In motion, and racing after the flabby man, Benson got to the car just as it screamed into motion. He caught the spare tire and hauled himself up onto the chrome bumper.

Fast as his body had moved in that crowded half-minute, his brain had worked still faster. He had perfected a plan, full-born, and was now following it. That was to let the flabby fellow get away—and follow him to whomever he reported to. He would probably go at once to some superior to report the fiasco here at the farm. Benson wanted very much to see who that superior was.

The mechanic didn't count. Obviously he was a day laborer in crime and knew nothing whatever of the sinister central plot of this business. So Benson had merely put him on ice with the flying hatchet handle.

Queer, he thought, how a man's personal history repeats itself. Those two, if they'd only known, had played into his hands by the choice of a hatchet as death weapon.

Benson had nearly been killed, in his teens, by a madman with a hatchet in Australia. He had used now the tactics that had instinctively saved his life then. And after the narrow escape in Australia, he had monkeyed with hatchets himself. He had learned to throw one so he could split a knot at thirty feet. He could throw an ax almost as accurately—

He saw a headlight approaching the swaying car which the flabby man was blindly driving with one broken arm limp by his side. He wondered who in the world that could be, approaching this desolate spot on a back road.

A second later he heard the flabby man scream, and felt the car swerve as he jammed the brakes. Instantly Benson released his hold and dropped to the lane. And less than two seconds later there was a crash that seemed to fill the quiet country night with sound for miles around.

Benson doubled catlike to his feet and leaped around the car.

It had been rammed by a taxicab, a thing looking odd and lonesome out here far from the city pavements. The cab, built like a truck for long life, as most cabs are, had plowed into the sedan so hard that the motor was shifted back on its mountings.

The driver of the sedan? The flabby man had been thrown against the windshield with such force that his head had gone through. And the windshield was of shatterproof glass!

There are a few times when shatterproof glass is worse than the old-fashioned kind. Such a time is when a person's head is forced through. Then, where ordinary glass would tend to crack clear out of the windshield, the nonshatterable kind remains intact, with just a head-sized hole in it. And the edges of the hole, around the victim's throat, become a jagged-edge guillotine!

Such had happened here. The driver's head bloomed through the windshield like some sort of monstrous growth. But the owner of the head would never move again. For the razorlike edges of the hole in the glass had bitten deep into his throat.

From the wrecked taxi, a man crawled gingerly. The man moved experimentally, then straightened, unhurt.

51

He was tall, bony, with great knobby hands and ears that stuck out like sails. MacMurdie.

He came forward and clutched Benson by the shoulders.

"Mon, ye're all right! Thank Heaven! When I saw this skurlie in the car comin' away from here, I thought they'd already done ye in and were makin' a getaway."

Benson stared at the Scot out of pale-gray eyes which were cold wells of frustration.

"How did you get here?" he said, lips barely moving with the clipped words, as was their habit now.

"I heard at the airport ye'd been taken away 'sick.' I knew what that meant, and had an idea where they'd take ye. So I followed. A mon at the airport fired after me in the cab. But when I'd got in, I'd put my hat high on my head, figurin' it might be a target, so the bullet only went through felt an inch above my scalp. A minute after, I took the whole cab and set the driver out, and came on here. But how is it ye come around from behind this car, without a scratch on ye? Weren't ye in it?"

Benson's gray-ice eyes went from the Scotchman's face.

MacMurdie had spoiled a promising plan. Benson was sure the flabby man would have led him to someone of importance in this great but still unguessable crime plot. And now, the flabby man, thanks to MacMurdie's red anger at the fear of his chief's death, had died himself. He'd be no good to anybody now. And the mechanic lying unconscious behind knew nothing.

But MacMurdie had had no way of knowing all that. He had acted out of loyalty, so, of course, there was nothing to be said to him.

"I was behind the car," was all Benson said. His eyes were again imperturbable in the white death of his face. "Come on, Mac. That automobile crash will be investigated, and it wouldn't be discreet for us to have the police find us."

"As long as ye weren't killed," said the Scot, "did ye find out anything?"

"Very little. My . . . wife and girl"—the cold, clipped words were almost steady—"were put out of the way so they couldn't witness something that went on in that plane. So much seems to have become clear. I would have been put out of the way, too, but I had a gun and they couldn't attack me till too late. So they did the next best thing and made up that fantastic story to clear themselves."

"But what was it they did in the plane?"

"I don't know." Benson's pale-gray eyes were grimly thoughtful. "They made only one slip, Mac. One of them mentioned either a man or a thing called 'Old Ironsides.'"

MacMurdie was thoughtful in his turn. Then he said: "'Tis a mon, I'm thinkin'. Someone big and influential in the city. I've heard the nickname. But I can't put my hand on it, quite."

"It would be someone big—and influential," nodded Benson. "That much, too, I gathered. For there's millions in it somewhere, and lives are not important. It is up to us to scuttle this thing and save those many lives."

CHAPTER VII

Murder on Wheels

Wallace Buell, junior partner in the brokerage firm of Carney & Buell, looked sympathetic. He was a brisk and businesslike man, forty-five, slightly bald, with gimlet black eyes and a professionally easy manner.

"I'd advise you to sell," he said.

He looked more sympathetic still. The firm of Carney & Buell was a big outfit, the Buffalo representatives of one of the biggest financial houses in New York. He had had to advise many clients, in his time, to sell when it meant a ruinous loss, but he could still look sympathetic about it.

"It seems to be the only wise course," he added.

The man he was talking to was Arnold Leon, a Buffalo manufacturer. Leon was sixty, slight, gray-haired and worried-looking. He protested vigorously.

"Sell my block of stock in Buffalo Tap & Die?" he said. "What kind of advice do you call that?"

"Good advice, as far as I can see it," Buell said. "We know all about Tap & Die. Our New York associates floated the stock issue in the Buffalo Tap & Die Works, as you know. We're quick to catch an unfavorable trend. The stock is down, and it's going lower, Mr. Leon. Sell!"

"According to the last annual report," Leon said worriedly, "Tap & Die has cash assets more than equal to their indebtedness. It's a sound company. Why should I sell the stock at a loss?"

"Here's one reason," said Buell. "No one knows it as yet but us. You know Lawrence Hickock?"

Leon nodded. "I know of him."

"Well, Lawrence Hickock, president of Tap & Die—can't be reached anywhere."

"What?"

"Yes." Buell's eyes were looking a little worried, too. "For three days, his whereabouts have been unknown. His friends don't know where he is. His family don't know. No one knows. He has just—skipped out! And when the head of a company mysteriously disappears, what is your natural conclusion?"

Arnold Leon chewed his lips.

"The natural conclusion is that something crooked has been going on, and that he fled before it should become known," he admitted.

"Exactly," said Buell. "Now, the stock is already far down below par. Suppose the papers get hold of Hickock's flight? That'll take the stock down so far it may even be removed from the board. I have sold what little I own—and I repeat, you'd be wise to sell, too."

Leon worried it out, waxen, elderly face twisted with the jitters.

"I put a lot of faith in your judgment," he said. "I've done business with you a long time. But, confound it, the cash reserve of Buffalo Tap & Die should meet any emergency. Suppose there has been crooked work. It could hardly be on such a large scale as to wreck the company. Suppose the stock does go way down. It'll come back, or ought to. I don't want to sell—"

Buell's private phone buzzed. Buell picked it up, then said, "Mr. Leon? Yes. Right here."

He handed the phone to Leon.

"Arnold?" came a voice. "This is John Lansing talking."

"Lansing!" Leon's voice was surprised. John Lansing was a Buffalo millionaire with a great deal of authority around the city, and with his fingers in most pies. "I thought you were in Florida."

"I was. Just got back this morning. And I've been

56

hearing some curious things about Tap & Die. Could you come and have a talk with me about it?"

"Gladly!" said Leon. "I'll be right around."

He hung up with an almost explosive sigh of relief.

"Lansing wants to talk it over," he said to Buell. "He owns a big block of stock, too. And he's as shrewd as they make 'em. It will be a relief to discuss the proposition with him."

Buell looked relieved, too.

"Lansing *is* a smart old duck," he said. "After your talk, drop me a hint of his advice, will you? I trust his judgment as much as your own, even though we're professional traders."

"I'll do it," nodded Leon.

He went out of the big ground-floor offices of Carney & Buell, past the customers' room where the board and its chalked quotations held the rigid attention of a score or so of men, and through the bronze revolving door.

At the curb was his car. It was a big town car of dark blue. In the front seat, immobile as a block of wood, was a gigantic figure of a man in black whipcord.

"To Mr. Lansing's home, Algernon," Leon said.

The chauffeur's huge face, moonlike and placid, with peaceable and not-too-intelligent-looking china-blue eyes, writhed a little with that "Algernon." But the giant only said, in a voice rather high for his vast bulk: "Mr. Lansing's home. Yes, sir."

The home of John Lansing, in the heart of the best residential section, squatted in half a block of lawn and looked like a bank. It seemed very quiet when you considered how many people must be around. All the servants, a family, friends. But not a soul could be seen as Leon's town car went up the front drive.

At the rear, there was a four-car garage with servants' quarters over it, and a covered tunnel into the house. No one moved out there, either.

"You're sure he's home, sir?" said the giant driver.

"Yes. Just got a phone call from him. Wait here, Algernon."

Leon, spruce and elderly and sober, trotted up the steps and rang the bell. The front door was opened. He stepped inside the house.

The minutes passed. Not one sound of activity came from the house. Not one glimpse of a living soul came from the grounds. The gigantic driver shifted uneasily at the wheel, and kept looking at the blank, dead door.

He opened the dash compartment and took out a thick book. "Radio-active Phenomena," the book was titled. He opened it near the back and began studying. But he could not keep his mind on the text.

An hour passed. And abruptly, with a shake of decision, the huge driver moved his vast shoulders and got out of the monkey seat. Something about this picture didn't smell right.

He went to the door and rang the bell. A butler would open it, of course, Leon would presently appear, and he'd bawl him out for being so fresh as to inquire for him. But the driver decided he'd take that chance. Every instinct told him something was wrong.

No one answered the ring. He punched at the bell again, heard it echo hollowly through vaulting space. You can *feel* if a place is untenanted.

But this place ought not to be empty! His boss had gone in there, hadn't he?

The chauffeur's placid eyes had taken on a queer, deep, alert look on his moon face. He put his hand on the ornate wrought-iron doorknob.

This man, for all the commonplace-looking chauffeur's livery, was like something that had stepped from the legendary age of giants. He was six feet nine. He weighed two hundred and eighty-five pounds. He was fifty-three inches around the chest, and wore a size-nineteen collar. His arms were bigger around than most men's thighs, and his legs were pillars fit for building-foundation purposes. Under his arms, among the barrel of his chest, the slabs and knots of muscle were so ponderous that his arms couldn't hang straight down—they crooked out so that they looked stubby, though actually they were almost of gorilla length.

Men of the giant's breed are seen occasionally. Primo Carnera was one such. But they are rare. And when they do happen along, the ordinary appliances and furnishings of life are not proportioned for them.

The giant shook the locked front door. Then, with a heave that threatened to burst the whipcord livery over his huge shoulders, he lunged inward.

The heavy front door thudded, stuck, then burst in, taking half the frame along with it. The big fellow stepped into a front hall. He loomed there—alone. And in the house was not a tick of sound.

"Hey!" he yelled.

No answer.

"Mr. Leon—"

He started forward, but stopped at the first doorway. The furniture inside was sheeted. So was the stuff in all the other rooms.

Only the hall was normal, with chairs uncovered. The house was closed. Lansing wasn't here. No one was. But Leon had been admitted by a man in livery.

The giant hurried with increasing speed from room to room. All were empty. His employer wasn't in that house. He raced to the back, along the covered tunnel to the garage, which backed on an alley. Reason told him that Leon had been taken out here. But instinct held a superstitious turn.

It was as if the man had stepped into that house—and in it vanished into thin air! The chauffeur raced back to the town car.

In the clear May sunlight, a small closed truck drove along the residential section. On its sides was lettered: "Buffalo Malt Products Co." A thin fellow with a cap pulled low and a cigarette dangling from a corner of a slack mouth was alone in the cab.

Behind, were three men. Two were of a piece with the ratlike driver. The third was Leon.

Leon lay on the floor of the truck, breathing heavily, face blue-white. One of the men was holding a soaked rag to his nose. The other suddenly grabbed it away.

"Hey! Easy on that chloroform. Don't croak the old goat!"

"Ah-h-h! So what? He'll probably get it anyway."

"Not for a while, he won't. The boss has got ideas about him."

The man with the rag was scowling, but he'd taken it away from Leon's nostrils.

"Sure," he complained. "Sure. The boss has ideas. But *what* ideas? Did it ever strike you that nobody ever tells us guys anything? The 'boss,' whoever he is, gives orders to do something, so we do it. He says not to do something, so we don't do it. But nobody ever whispers a word of what it's all *about*."

The other man looked actually frightened for a minute.

"Shut up, you dummy! This is one play where it ain't wise to know too much. It's big. A big shot or two's behind it. There's plenty of protection. That's all we need to know."

"It ain't all *I* need. I like to have a foot in the door when I do things. I don't like to play 'em blind."

The other man was silent a moment, ratlike eyes on his pal's face.

"The last guy talked like that," he said finally, "got picked up in a ditch with a couple pounds of lead in him. This is so big nobody's supposed to ask questions."

"I'll take my chances," the other said arrogantly. "I'm going to nose around and find out some things. You wait and see!"

His pal glanced through the small window ahead, and saw over the driver's shoulder, through the windshield, that the little truck was coasting along a street where vacant lots were the rule and houses the exception. He whirled back.

"Pete!" croaked the man with the rag suddenly, voice hoarse.

He stared into the automatic that had appeared in Pete's hand.

"Pete—"

The gun moved forward a little.

"Pete . . . I didn't mean it! I don't care what's behind this. I won't try to find out anything."

Pete was silent.

"You can't do a thing like this, Pete! Why, we're pals. We been together for six years. We did time together. Now you can't rub me out just because—"

The gun jabbed forward still farther.

The explosion, muffled by the man's clothes and body, wasn't loud. The noise of the truck helped muffle it. And anyhow, there was no one around on that outlying street to hear.

The man sagged, with the chloroform rag dropping from his limp hand. He died staring at Pete's face, unbelievingly, pleadingly. And Pete stared back with his mouth working.

In Pete's eyes could be read regret—but also a fear of somebody or something so great that it made even the murder of an old pal a thing to be committed without question if that pal got nosy.

The truck went on, bearing the dead gunman and the unconscious rich man.

CHAPTER VIII

Mike and Ike

Benson was in his suite at the Hotel Ely. MacMurdie, who had been given a room adjoining, was in there, too. Benson was opening the small, heavy package MacMurdie had picked up for him yesterday.

The man with the still, white face took two things from a mass of wrappings. One was a knife, the other a gun. But they were like no knife or gun the dour Scot had ever seen before.

The knife was about eight inches long over all, and had practically no handle. The blade was double-edged, with a reinforcing spine down the middle. When Benson titled the weapon a bit, MacMurdie saw that the handle was a light, hollow tube.

"It's a throwing knife I designed myself," said Benson, lips barely moving with the words. He stared at the thing, eyes like frosty steel, face as dead as a mask of ice. "Heavy in the blade, light in the handle. Look."

Benson held the knife, handle down, about shoulder-high, and dropped it. In midair the blade overbalanced the handle and came down point first. Even that short drop was enough to sink it lightly into the floor, so sharp was the point and so easily did it needle into the carpet.

Benson picked it up again and, it seemed without really looking, threw it. His arm didn't even draw all the way back. It lashed forward in an abbreviated arc. And the knife, with a deadly swish, snipped a coat button off MacMudie's breast, over his heart, and went on to sink two inches into the wood of the door a yard beyond.

63

"I've gone a little rusty," Benson said. "But then it's been three years since I used it—ten since a Javanese taught me the trick in Singapore. I'll pick it up again."

He took up the gun.

It was a .22, but that, the caliber, was the only thing standard about it. The barrel was almost as long as the barrel of a target pistol. The cylinder, to streamline the gun, was small and held only four cartridges. The butt slanted so that it was almost in a straight line with the barrel. Altogether, it was almost like a straight piece of blued steel tubing with a little bulge for a cylinder and a slight bend for a handle.

There was a silencer on it.

"I've never seen the like of them before," said Mac-Murdie, staring at the two weapons.

"You'll probably never see the like again," Benson replied, clipped words sliding from immobile lips.

He rolled his trousers legs up to the knee. To the inside of the left calf he strapped a slim sheath, and in it he slid the razor-sharp knife. To the inside of the right calf, so that it conformed to the bulge of steely muscle there, he strapped an almost-as-slim holster into which he slipped the tiny gun.

"Mike and Ike," he said, pale-gray eyes glittering with a deadly light. "Mike's the gun. Ike's the knife. They are true friends. They've saved my life a great many times. I'd thought I'd never need them again. But they come back into active service now."

"Mon, ye couldn't kill fast enough with that popgun, stacked against a .45, we'll say. The big one would blast ye to bits before the little one could sting enough to take life."

"I don't kill with Mike," retorted Benson. But he didn't bother to explain at the moment.

"So the cab driver who took me and my wife to the airport that day can't be traced," he said.

"Right," nodded MacMurdie glumly. "If he's in town, he's hidin' out. He's driving no cabs now."

"I rather thought he'd be missing. They're cleaning up the loose ends, Mac. The driver was a loose end. I, or some investigator in my employ, might get to him—and he might eventually talk. So he has been put out of the way. But the lead I got has turned into something."

"Ye mean what ye heard the mon say in the car that took you to the farmhouse? The words, 'Old Ironsides'?"

"Yes," said Benson. "I found out who Old Ironsides is. He's Lawrence Hickock, a wealthy Buffalo businessman. He is president of a firm called the Buffalo Tap & Die Works. His nickname comes from his sideburns, old-fashioned, iron-gray, bushy."

He walked to the closet, a lithe gray wolf of a man with only his deadly pale eyes alive in his white, dead face. He put on the hat that was subtly reinforced with wire to take and hold any shape he chose to give it. He donned the light spring topcoat that, at a second's notice, would be altered to look like an entirely different garment.

"We progress, though slowly," he told the Scot. "So far, we know this: The gang behind this has booked the Montreal plane several times to carry something no one is supposed to know anything about. That object—or those objects—went in the trunk invariably accompanying the gang. At a certain spot it was taken from the trunk and dropped. Because they didn't dare have my wife and child see what was dropped through the trapdoor, they . . . threw them out of the plane first, that night."

MacMurdie was no yes-man. He shook his dour head.

"If they wanted to drop something some place, they would hire a private plane, wouldn't they? Why take chances with a big public transport plane?"

"There's an answer for that, too. They had several things to drop. That meant several trips. A chartered plane, going out quite a few times to the same spot, could be observed and perhaps questions asked about it. But no one would ever question the regular flight of a regular plane over a commercial route. It was smarter and less traceable to use that transport than to hire a plane."

He went to the door. "Stay here for calls, Mac." The brief agony that touched Benson's eyes was a terrible thing. But the white, still face reflected no expression at all. "I'm still hoping there may be a ransom demand for Alicia and the girl. You'll be here if it comes."

"Ye're going to see this mon, Hickock?"

"Yes," said Benson, and went out with his lithe, smooth tread.

A call to Hickock's office had disclosed the fact that he was not there. So Benson went to the magnate's home.

Old Ironsides, named by the member of that gang! Was the man, so respected in town, so well-to-do, one of the powers behind this plot? Or was he a victim?

It soon developed that he was the latter. A victim!

A middle-aged woman with frantic brown eyes came to the door when Benson asked to see Mr. Hickock.

"You have word?" she said, voice trembling near hysteria. "You have word from my husband?"

"Isn't he here?" countered Benson.

Mrs. Hickock stared at the dead face, looked deep into the fog-gray eyes. Then over her own eyes a veil seemed to lower.

"He isn't at home just now," she said, voice brittle and controlled with great effort.

"Do you know when he will return?"

"Soon, I imagine. I can take any message you have to give, and tell him when he comes. Is it personal or a business call?"

Benson's pale eyes were boring into the veiled brown ones. They could read closed books, those eyes. Though, at that, this human document was not too closed.

Hickock not at home. His wife wild about it. Asking if he "had word" of her husband. It spelled a single sinister word—one that rends all the emotions and is usually hidden from the police till too late.

Kidnap!

"It's a business call," he said evenly. "I'll come again, later."

No use trying to question Mrs. Hickock. She'd refuse to answer while she had her composure, be too hysterical to answer coherently if questioning were pressed. Benson left.

But he only went as far as the corner.

There, he took out a small mirror and altered the lines of the dead flesh of his face. He had come as himself. Now he became a man with lean cheeks and heavy jowls, lips straight and a little cruel over a jaw with a bulbous tip. He turned the brim of his hat down in front, up high at sides and rear, so that it looked like something a fisherman ashore on a vacation might wear. He slipped into the topcoat wrong side out and presented a gaudy check to the world.

He went back to the Hickock grounds, and passed by the house. A groundsman was working at a flower plot near the garage. He went up to the man. At the rear window, the servant who had admitted Benson to see Mrs. Hickock looked out and saw him, but didn't recognize him at all as the fellow who had just left.

The groundsman glanced at him, eyes curious at the interruption to his work.

"Well?" he said.

Benson said: "I came out here to get a little more information, if I can, about your employer, Mr. Hickock."

The man just stared at him, face secretive. It was plain that he could keep his own counsel, and that of his employer.

"They tell me," Benson went on, "that you were one of the last around here to see Mr. Hickock before he left the other day—and didn't come back."

"Who told you?" said the man suspiciously.

Benson jerked his head toward the big house. The man drew the natural conclusion. His face lost its guarded secretiveness. Something like relief came into his eyes.

"Oh! So they've decided at last to tell the cops, and you were sent out! That's good. I don't think people ought to keep these things quiet."

"Very dangerous to," agreed Benson. "Tell me what you know of the disappearance, will you?"

"I suppose they've told you most of it in the house," the man said, shrugging his shoulders. "Three mornings ago, Mr. Hickock left for the office. But on the way he was going to stop off at the home of Mr. John Lansing. Mr. Lansing called at breakfast and asked him to. Anyhow, that's what the second maid says. Mr. Hickock left, driving his own car, and that was the last of him."

"He didn't get to the office after the call to Mr. Lansing?"

"Nope. He left here—and disappeared, that's all. But the call from Mr. Lansing must have been a stall. I hear they've called there a dozen times. There's nobody home. Mr. Lansing himself is down in Florida, and has been for three months. His house seems to be all shut up."

"They certainly delayed about calling the police," said Benson expressionlessly.

The man shrugged again.

"You know how it is. His family's wild. His friends and the guys who work for him are nuts. But everybody's afraid to say a word to the cops for fear it'll go hard with Old Ironsides. They're just sittin' around waiting for a ransom demand, I guess. Far's I know, none has come yet."

"So he went to John Lansing's home," Benson repeated.

He left, to go there himself.

He arrived just as a big town car with a giant of a man in chauffeur's livery at the wheel, swirled out of the drive and began going like a comet away from the place. He took the car's number.

Five minutes later, after observing the wrecked front door of Lansing's place and confirming the report that the place was closed and tenantless, he phoned the

68

motor bureau and found that the town car belonged to Arnold Leon.

Fifteen minutes later his car, a fast roadster he'd bought early that morning, slid to a stop in front of the Leon residence. He saw the town car in front of the garage and as he went toward it, he saw the huge chauffeur hurrying from the rear door of the house, shedding his livery coat as he walked.

Benson stopped in front of him. "Just a minute," he said.

The man stopped and stared down at him.

Thirteen years before, in Alaska, Benson had known a man called Bull Red. He was just under seven feet tall, with a leonine mane of red hair, and bent crowbars with his bare hands without bothering to brace them over his knee. Not since the days of Bull Red had Benson seen such size as he saw now, in this chauffeur.

"All right, what do you want?" snapped the huge fellow, holding his coat over his arm.

"You're the chauffeur for Mr. Leon?" Benson said.

There was black fury in the giant's eyes. And something else. The ordinary person would see in the big fellow a moon-faced guy with mild china-blue eyes who was as stupid as he was enormous. But Benson saw deeper. He saw a fast brain concealed under the phlegmatic, full face, and plenty of intelligence in the far depths of the china-blue eyes.

"I *was* the driver for Mr. Leon," the man snapped. "I was just fired!"

"Oh?" said Benson. "You mean, when you got back from Lansing's house?"

The giant glared. "How do you know I was there? And what's it to you?"

"I know you were there because I saw you," said Benson calmly. "And it's this to me: there's a mystery about that house and I want to solve it."

The giant crouched a little, as if the words had been blows.

"So!" he said. "You're a cop! Well, you won't get *me* for the boss' disappearance!"

He leaped at Benson as he spoke.

Benson had been sure, on eyeing all that vast bulk, that the man would be so muscle-bound that he'd have about the agility of a snowplow. Bull Red had been slowed by being muscle-bound. But this man jumped at him as swiftly and certainly as if he'd been a flyweight boxer!

Fast as Benson was himself, he had time only to get his right hand up, and jerk his head to one side as a fist like a side of beef swept by. It was lucky he got the hand up for the giant's vast hand caught his left shoulder.

The big fellow had time for only one short press of his huge fingers, but that almost did for the fast gray fox of a man with the dead, still face. Then Benson's free right hand got a fold of flesh and muscle under the giant's extended left armpit in a police grip that is warranted to make any man howl. He twisted with his steel-wire fingers.

The big fellow gasped and let go. Benson's hand shot up from the armpit to the column of a throat. He bent his back like a fast gray cat, and the giant rolled over it like an avalanche and crashed to the graveled drive.

It would have done for most, but this man got up as lithely as if he'd weighed a third what he actually did. He flashed for Benson again, less recklessly this time, with the black fury higher in his eyes—but with something like respect there, too.

From the house behind them some woman was screaming.

"Police! Get the police! He kidnapped my father! Now he's murdering somebody! *Police!*"

Benson feinted from the tremendous arms that were reaching for him; but fast as he was, the big fellow was almost as fast. He got Benson's right wrist in a bone-crushing grip, and twisted his arm up behind him.

Then he put his right arm, as huge as a flexible tree trunk, around Benson with his doubled fist in the middle of his back and began breaking the gray man with the dead, white face in two.

Quality in muscle, as well as quantity! The giant weighed nearly twice as much as Benson, and he was putting forth his full strength in an effort to crack Benson's spine. But into the gray man's steel cables of sinew surged the explosive, mysterious power that makes the muscle fiber of a rare few far superior, ounce for ounce, to that of ordinary men.

For a few seconds he actually stopped that appalling pressure on his back. Like a steel bar, bending thus far and no farther, he quivered there in the big man's crushing grip. But it could only last a few seconds, and Benson knew it. So he risked everything on a single throw.

Deliberately exposing himself even more to the terrible pressure, he twisted enough to get his left arm loose, and brought his hand up to the back of the giant's neck. There, with blackness fogging his brain and with his final reserve of strength almost gone, he pressed deep on either side of the spinal column with thumb and second finger.

For a full five seconds the giant made no sound, and there was no slackening of his terrific grip. Benson, with the black fog almost overwhelming him, and with his own muscles failing perceptibly, wondered in a dim corner of his brain at the giant's resistance to that deadly grip. Was that vast bulk made of metal? Were there no ropes of nerves there, as in other men, to cut off consciousness as they were pressed?

Then, all at once, like a falling tree, the big fellow sagged. His arms slid from their hold, and he slumped to his knees, shaking his head like a stricken bull to clear his vision.

Benson reeled to the town car and leaned against a fender to get his own strength back. And in the silence, the screams of the woman from the house were apparent to the ears of both once more.

"Police! Police!"

The big fellow spoke, kneeling in the gravel, staring with utter unbelief at the comparatively small man who had beaten him, staring with something like awe at the white, set face which even now expressed no emotion whatever.

"You're the only man," he said hoarsely, "who ever got away from me, once I got my hands on him!"

Panting, Benson didn't answer. It had been the nearest thing in his life. He concentrated on getting his strength back.

"All right," the big fellow said, getting to legs that shook under him like uncertain tree trunks. "You can take me in. Any cop that can do that to me—"

"I'm not a cop," said Benson.

"You're not?" said the giant. "Why, I thought you'd trailed me here to arrest me because my boss, Leon, disappeared from the house where I'd driven him—"

"Leon gone?" Benson snapped, straightening. "Your employer, too? Is every influential person in the city menaced by this thing? Tell me what you can—"

"All right. But make it some place else, fast," said the giant, "before the cops do come in answer to Miss Leon's screaming. Because if they come, they'll get me for the boss' disappearance—and they'll make it stick!"

CHAPTER IX

Smitty Joins Up

The giant was bursting out of the largest ready-made suit Benson had been able to get in Buffalo. But it would have to do till a tailor could make up a suit to order.

"Or maybe 'tis a tent maker we'll have to call in for ye," said MacMurdie, frosty blue eyes traveling over the great body.

The three were in Benson's hotel suite. Benson was staring with gray gimlet eyes at the giant's mild-seeming china-blue ones.

"Your employer just walked into that house, belonging to John Lansing, and didn't come out again?" Benson repeated.

The big fellow nodded.

"And you came back in a hurry and reported it to his daughter, and she hysterically discharged you, and indicated that she was going to hand you over to the police."

"Yes," said the giant, voice too high for his bulk.

"Why was she so sure you had something to do with the kidnaping? For kidnaping's what it must have been."

The big fellow reddened. "Because I've been in jail," he said defiantly.

Benson's gray eyes probed deep. He didn't see the sly shrewdness of the criminal in the china-blue eyes. All he saw was a huge fellow, a lot smarter than he appeared to be, who would be as decent a citizen as anyone else— unless he were roused.

"Care to explain the jail sentence?" he said.

73

"I was framed," said the giant. "It was with a big electrical-equipment corporation. I'm an electrical engineer. Graduated from Massachusetts Tech. I was working on television, and some platinum disappeared from the laboratory. Eight thousand dollars' worth. They nailed *me* for it, and I got a year in the pen. I'd have gotten ten, only the evidence was so clouded the conviction wasn't clear. I couldn't get a regular job after that. All I could get was a job as chauffeur to Mr. Leon, who overlooked my past. Then something has to go and happen to him! If I'm ever tagged as the last man to see him alive, with my jail record, I'll go up for kidnaping as sure as there's a ceiling over our heads."

"That's why you charged at me the minute I opened my mouth to ask you a question?"

"That's why. I thought you were a cop and I didn't dare let a cop take me."

"What's your name?"

The giant stared at the pale-gray eyes with his ears slowly reddening.

"Algernon Heathcote Smith," he said in a stifled voice.

MacMurdie stared at the almost three hundred pounds of brawn with his frosty blue eyes widening. Then for the first time Benson heard him laugh.

"Algie!" the Scot hooted. "Algie! Heathcote! Why—"

The giant's body rippled toward him, and MacMurdie became discreetly silent. The big fellow faced Benson again.

"The name's Smitty to my friends," he said. And he added dangerously, "Most people try to be friends with me."

"I wouldn't doubt it," said Benson, ice-gray eyes traveling over the unbelievable mountain of sinew. "So you're out of a job, Smitty. And you can drive, and you're an electrical engineer with enough technical training to be working on television. Would you like to work for me? I think I could use you."

"I'd like it very much."

"*Whoosh*, chief!" exclaimed MacMurdie. "We don't need the help of little boys. You and I can—"

Smitty's ingenuous blue eyes went his way again, and MacMurdie once more relapsed into thoughtful silence.

"What work is it you want me to do?" Smitty asked the gray man with the immobile white face.

"Dangerous work," said Benson. "I wouldn't blame you if you decided against taking it when you've heard about it. We're fighting against some organized gang of criminals so daring that men like your employer, Leon, and like Lawrence Hickock, seem menaced—along with Heaven knows how many lesser lives. A gang so powerful that the police seem helpless to hold any of the lesser killers turned in to them. A gang so clever that even now, after strenuous efforts, we hardly know more concerning their eventual murderous goal than we did when we started out. Quite possibly one or all of us may be killed before we're through. That's the work, Smitty. Care to take it on?"

The giant's moon-full face with the china-blue eyes, for once, expressed the keen intelligence and firm will that dwelt behind the not-very-bright-looking exterior.

"I'd count it a rare privilege to help you in such work, sir," he said. "And now, if you wouldn't mind telling me more—"

Benson told the story from the start, eyes like tortured gray steel in a face that could not move a muscle to express the agony of recounting that dreadful starting episode in the plane. And Smitty listened with fury and sympathy to the clipped words of his new chief.

Mystery can work in opposite directions. If Benson had been unable to get far, as yet, toward the core of the grim mystery that had been exploded into his life with the disappearance of wife and child, so, too, had the men against whom he was fighting been unable to penetrate the mystery of who was beginning to get so close to their mongrel heels.

Pete, from the light truck that had borne Leon away

to an unknown destination, and the slack-lipped driver of that truck, still with his inevitable cigarette drooping from the corner of his loose mouth, talked it over a bit.

They were in a cheap boardinghouse room kept in Pete's name.

"It's that guy, Benson, of course, who's behind the monkeyin' around," Pete said. "But where's Benson keeping himself? Benson's a black-haired young fella. All we've seen around is a white-haired guy with a face like something dug up from a grave at midnight. I tell you, the boss is getting kinda worried about it."

"Who *is* the boss?" mused the slack-lipped driver.

Pete turned baleful eyes on him. The man hastily backtracked.

"Look, I ain't sayin' I'm going to nose around and find out things—like the guy you had to knock off in the truck. I'm just a little curious—see? Don't get me wrong. If you know anything about this, and feel like talking, go ahead. If you don't, I don't care. Get me?"

"I don't know a thing," Pete said, relaxing stiffly. "That's the truth."

"You don't know the answer to all this stuff we've been doing?"

"No. Snatch. That's all I know. But—nobody's had the bee put on 'em for money yet. It beats me."

"And you don't know who's behind it?"

"No, and I don't want to. It's unhealthy. Anybody in the crowd gets a grand for opening up anybody else who gets too nosy. That's a standing offer. When it's like that—you think I'm going around investigating?"

Pete lit a cigarette and drew deep.

"Now, this white-haired guy who has been gettin' so busy—" he began.

His phone rang. He picked it up.

"S404," a voice said. All you could tell about the voice, so muffled and disguised was it, was that it was that of a man. But the code number—of a plane—was right.

"O.K. shoot," Pete said tersely.

"Go to the home of Mrs. Martineau," the muffled voice rapped out. "Others are going to the homes of the rest. You will do as they are ordered to do: Watch the place. Don't be seen. Watch from a distance. Any man going there to investigate—see that he doesn't get far alive. You understand?"

"I understand. You want I should go alone?"

"Take another with you. The man we're beginning to want out of the way is clever. But two of you should be able to handle him."

"I'll say we'll be able to handle him!" Pete said, lips in a cold grin. "O.K., boss."

He hung up. The other man stared.

"Say! Was that the boss? Was—"

"I don't know," Pete snapped. "That's the way we get all our orders. Just a guy over the phone. I don't know who he is. Come on."

"Where to?"

"The joint where the widow Martineau lives—or lived! The big shots are worried that Benson may get wind of what happened to her, and go snoopin' around her place. If he does—"

Pete took out his automatic, looked at the full clip, and slipped the safety off and then on again in answer.

Back at the Hotel Ely, Benson was studying the latest editions of the newspapers. So was the giant, Smitty. But Benson was reading financial pages with his eyes like devouring gray flame, while Smitty was concentrating on the regular news.

The giant laid down the last paper with a sigh.

"There's no mention of the cops being after one Algernon Heathcote Smith," he said. "I believe it's as you predicted it would be: Leon's daughter stopped calling for the cops right after we left. She is now kept silent by the same fear that holds in all such cases. She's afraid if she reports anybody to the police—me or anybody else—it will go hard with her father. I guess it will be all right for me to walk around loose for a while."

Benson simply nodded. He was studying the financial news that had been repeated in one form or another by all the papers.

The news was local—and had to do with the Buffalo Tap and Die Works.

For the past twenty-four hours it has been impossible for anyone to get in touch with Mr. Stephen Vincent, secretary-treasurer to Buffalo Tap & Die. He has gone away "for a week's rest," according to members of his family and employees near to him. In the opinion of this humble correspondent, that seems highly unusual when you consider that for some time past, it has been impossible to get in touch with Mr. Lawrence Hickock, president of the same firm. The unexplained absence of two high officers of this concern seems to hint that perhaps an investigation of finances should be in order. Where is the much vaunted S.E.C. in this matter?

And in another part of the same paper, under "Financial Transactions," the following caught the pale-gray eyes:

The extensive holdings of Mrs. Robert Martineau, widow of Dollar Martineau, in Buffalo Tap & Die Works, were thrown on the falling market for that stock with the opening bell this morning. It further added to the chaos of the unfortunate firm's affairs. Insiders are trying to guess what is in the wind—

Benson looked at the stock quotations, deadly pale eyes like swords of ice in his dead face.

The stock of Buffalo Tap & Die, par 100, was down to 14.

Benson got up, a flashing gray fox methodically and swiftly weaving one cold trail after another into a straight path on which the scent was growing warm. Smitty towered anxiously over him.

"Going somewhere, chief? Let me go for you, huh? You haven't given me anything to do. You've got that redheaded Scotchman out at the Buffalo airport snooping around. But you haven't given *me* a job."

"You'll get plenty, Smitty." The clipped words came from lips as still and set as gray stone. Meanwhile, Benson was at work before the mirror.

His fingers, growing ever more deft at their almost gruesome job, were manipulating the strangely dead flesh of his white face.

The set lips went up a little in a reckless, happy-go-lucky cast. The features were shaped into a lean and cynical mask. One eyebrow went up a fraction of an inch higher than the other.

Benson put on the hat and bent brim and crown into shapelessness. He put on the topcoat and left the collar up a little, sloppily.

Smitty suddenly nodded. "I get it. A reporter."

"Yes," said Benson. "There may be danger where I'm going. Men posted to block investigation. If I can slip into the place and out again as an ordinary reporter, I may avoid trouble."

"If there's a chance of trouble," said Smitty, "there is also a chance that you might not come back. If you don't, in a specified time, where shall I go to look for you?"

"I'm going to Mrs. Robert Martineau's home. If I'm not back in an hour, follow me there."

Benson went out, with the giant's eyes still anxious on his new boss. Benson seemed a figure of ice more than a man. His face was like something resurrected from death. Not once had he shown a human emotion. Yet there was something about the man that had roused Smitty's instant and instinctive obedience. He felt he'd go through fire and flood for him. And he was worried about his safety now!

Had he known the trap set at the Martineau home, nothing could have kept the giant from going along.

CHAPTER X

Crime Plans Anew

Three miles from the outskirts of the city, in a ten-acre estate so well kept that it looked more like a public park than a private place, was the home of Mrs. Martineau.

The grounds were so wooded that the big house could not be seen from the road. There was a hundred yards of driveway, curving at the end to stop in a big circle before a front door as elaborate as that of a museum.

At this door three or four reporters tried to get into the house. There were not as many reporters as there would have been if personal tragedy were hinted. This was only a financial business, so financial reporters were here, and were not too tough about entrance.

A white-faced, agitated-looking servant was denying them all chances of an interview.

"Mrs. Martineau won't see you, gentlemen. She won't see anyone. She is not well. She hasn't seen anyone for several days. It seems to me it's her own business if she wants to sell—or buy—some stock or other on the market. Please go away, gentlemen."

"We'll go, as far as the drive," said the youngest of the men. "There we'll camp awhile. We want a few words with Mrs. Martineau on Buffalo Tap & Die. If she has any inkling of future movements—it's news."

"I've told you, Mrs. Martineau won't talk to anyone—"

Another man came up to the group. The stamp of the reporter was on him, though his face seemed paler than that of most of the boys who hoof it out in rain and sun, and though his eyes were a little colder than most.

The harrassed butler stared at him.

"You, too," he said. "You can't come in. No one can. Mrs. Martineau gave strict orders not to be disturbed."

Benson stared at the servant, at the door, and at the reporters.

"O.K.," he said, after a moment, with a shrug.

He walked back down the drive—and darted off to the left among concealing shrubbery as soon as he was out of sight of the front door. He doubled back to the house, to the side. He could hear the arguing voices in front as he went up a big maple tree, hand over hand, to a branch almost touching a third-floor window.

He went out on the branch, with the sure-footed tread of a great panther, and in through the window.

At the front door one of the financial reporters said: "Who's the guy with the poker face? I never saw *him* before."

"Don't work on any of the Buffalo sheets," another said.

Their voices carried. The words were heard by two men kneeling down low in a small screened summerhouse so that they could not be seen above the waist-high railing. The two had their guns out. They looked at each other significantly as they heard the words.

But Pete and his pal had not needed to hear. They had seen the newcomer double back to the house and climb in the high window, and had already guessed that he wasn't what he appeared.

Both rested their automatics on the rail of the little summerhouse, with the sights lined up on that window. Like that, with murderous eyes on the entrance which should also be the exit of their intended victim—they waited.

In the house, Benson stole with the silence of a cat toward the stairs, and down to the second floor. He could hear subdued, frantic voices from some room there. He got to the door of the room within which was the talking. He could only hear voices; not words. He soundlessly opened the door an inch, and looked in.

It was a large bedroom, with the western sun streaming in on two occupants. One was an old man with a seamed, anxious face. The other was a young woman whose status in the house was difficult to place. She was better dressed than a servant, and not as well dressed as a guest or relative. Secretary to Mrs. Martineau, Benson judged.

"What are we going to *do*?" said the girl, voice shaking.

The old man sighed. "I don't know. But I do know there is one thing we *can't* do. That is, to let anyone—above all, newspaper reporters—know that Helen isn't here."

"Where in the world do you suppose Mrs. Martineau is?"

The old man shook his head.

"You know as well as I do that something terrible has happened to my niece. Ten days, it has been, since we heard from her. She has been . . . carried away, somewhere, by someone."

"But what for? Ransom?"

"I don't know. We've had no demands. Perhaps there will be one later. I don't know."

Benson turned and left the door. He'd learned all he needed to know—had learned what he had suspected before.

It wasn't that Mrs. Martineau was ill that she refused to be seen. No one could talk to her—because she wasn't at this house to be talked to! Like Hickock, and Leon, she had disappeared off the face of the earth.

A third person of wealth and importance! A person, like the others, who the average crook wouldn't dare to touch!

Benson got to the window he had entered. But after a little pause, he did not go out. He went down more stairs instead.

"When you go into a place where you have the least

83

suspicion of bein' watched, son, *don't come out the same hole you went in!*"

A so-called Arizona bad man, whose "badness" usually resulted in the death of somebody long overripe for death, had tipped Benson to that little piece of advice years ago, when Benson was still in his teens but was taking his place just the same as a grown man in a tough country.

Benson calmly walked down the main hall of the big house to the front door. He opened the portal. The back of the arguing servant was toward him. The reporters gaped.

"Well, what do you know!" exclaimed one.

The servant whirled, saw Benson, and squealed:

"How dare you enter this house against orders? And how did you get in, anyway? If someone let you in the back door, after all the commands—"

His voice was interrupted by a double roar of heavy-caliber automatics, sounding almost as one. A .45 slug spat into stone within three inches of Benson's head. At the same time one of the reporters gave a scream of pain and sagged to the ground, where he clawed at his leg, from which blood was spouting from a hole above the knee.

Had Benson come out the window, where the two men had their guns trained as accurately as though held in a testing vise, he would have died. As it was, reappearing suddenly and unexpectedly from the point least foreseen by Pete and his pal, their hastily aimed guns had missed. And they got no second shots.

Benson, with the first bark of the heavy automatics, had leaped to one side and was gone, behind a bank of bushes. He whipped Ike, the slim, razorlike throwing dagger from its sheath below his left knee, and slashed off a branch of one of the bushes. He threw the branch. It hit in another clump of bushes thirty feet farther on.

"There he is," yelled a voice from the door, as the far clump of bushes quivered with the thrown branch.

And in the little summerhouse, Pete and the other gun-

84

man jerked their automatics toward that bush. Benson slipped Mike, the tiny, silenced .22 from its leg sheath. He aimed with care, but only for a half-second, and squeezed the trigger.

There was a soft *spat,* hardly louder than the *phutt* of an air gun. And Pete, with two inches of head showing above the summerhouse rail, went down. His companion stared at him with his mouth open. What had hit Pete? And from where?"

Blood trickled slowly down Pete's forehead from above the hairline. The other man stared around in terror— then went down himself as there was a second soft *spat* from Mike.

Benson, with the woodcraft of an Indian, stole from the spot and from the grounds unseen.

"So you killed them both," said Smitty, back at the hotel. Benson had returned well before the mentioned hour. Smitty's eyes were wholly approving as he said the words.

"I didn't kill them," said Benson, face still and calm as a snow-whitened pond. "I merely left them unconscious, for the police to take for the wounding of that reporter. I creased them, if you know what that means."

Smitty nodded.

"When a bullet hits a man a glancing blow on the top of his head, instead of drilling the head itself, that man is knocked cold instead of being killed. He is 'creased.' I've heard of it, but always as a freak accident. I didn't know anyone was good enough with a gun to shoot that fine on purpose."

Benson shrugged a little.

"Any man who can hit a dime at fifty paces can do it. It's not too difficult."

"It sounds miraculous to me," said the giant. "But— why *didn't* you kill them? They certainly deserved it."

Benson's ice-gray eyes narrowed.

"Ever kill a man, Smitty?"

"No."

"Well, I had to, once. In Tahiti. I swore I'd never kill again, if I could possibly avoid it. And to help avoid it, I practiced with Mike till I could hit that dime at that fifty paces."

Benson's eyes changed expression. His face could not change; it was a dead thing. So the gray flame of his pale, deadly eyes seemed to be gaining more expressiveness than eyes ordinarily have, in compensation.

He stared at Smitty.

"Any phone calls while I was gone?"

The giant shook his head. "Were you expecting any?"

"Expecting?" said Benson, tortured words slipping from lips that showed no torture. "No, Smitty. Hoping? Yes. I am still hoping that my wife and girl are alive. I am still hoping I'll get a demand for money in exchange for their lives. If I do—well, I have several million dollars, and the crooks can have it all, if they give Alicia and Alice back to me. After that—I'll wind them up or die trying! But first they can have all I've got if they'll return those two, alive."

"There was no phone call," said Smitty gently.

The door opened, and MacMurdie came in. The dour Scot was much excited about something.

"Reportin' from the airport," he said, with his Scotch burr more pronounced than ever. "There's things afoot, Muster Benson. New devilry."

The pale-gray eyes drilled into MacMurdie's frosty blue ones.

"The crowd that was on the plane with you that night have booked the same plane again tonight—for Montreal," said Mac.

Benson's body was as still as his face. Smitty stared at the Scot and then whistled. MacMurdie said:

"Another trip with . . . something . . . bound for . . . somewhere, I'm thinkin'. The plane with the trapdoor. Now what'll be dropped tonight?"

"A man," said Benson, voice as even and expressionless as his features. "That's what will be dropped. And I think the man will be Leon, your ex-employer, Smitty!"

CHAPTER XI

The Trapdoor Plane

Benson summed it up.

"Lawrence Hickock is gone, and no one knows where. Arnold Leon has disappeared. Mrs. Martineau the same —she has been missing even longer than Hickock. According to the newspapers, Stephen Vincent has also vanished. Perhaps others have, too. All those people seem to have one common connection. They either own stock in, or run, the Buffalo Tap & Die Works."

Benson continued: "The gang that takes over the Buffalo-Montreal plane periodically is connected with those disappearances, so I think we can accept almost as proven fact the theory that the gang kidnaps these wealthy, influential people and, one by one, drops them through the trapdoor of that plane to some unknown destination. That is what is carried aboard in the trunk each trip—a living, human body. That is what is dropped. And that is why they had to dispose of my wife and girl. The gang didn't dare have a living soul witness what went out that trapdoor."

"You mean, they just drop them?" said MacMurdie, blue eyes blazing. "Or do ye think they use parachutes?"

"Parachutes, I think," said Benson. "There would seem to be no point in going to such elaborate lengths just to kill their victims by dropping them in Lake Ontario. There are far easier ways to murder. No, they must 'chute the victims down, and hold them alive somewhere. And tonight, you say, Mac, the gang has booked the Montreal plane for one more run?"

"That's right, Muster Benson."

"Well, we've gone at least a little way in our journey of vengeance. I think we can go a little distance further and make a good guess at where the victims are dropped."

Benson opened a large map and pored over it with face bleak and white and dead but gray eyes alive. The map was of the eastern Great Lakes region. He pointed to the head of Lake Ontario, with Canada on one side and the United States on the other.

"I have figured the speed of the plane as well as I could," he said, clipped words rattling from still, immobile lips, "and I think the ship was about over the Thousand Islands region when I last saw my wife and girl. The Thousand Islands! There's a labyrinth for you! In that wilderness of water and rock, a hundred hiding places might be found where a gang would be safe from the law indefinitely. That is where I think our eventual goal lies. That is where I believe these missing persons are being held. Always assuming they aren't dead, of course."

MacMurdie, the careful Scot, went to the map with his lips pursed. No yes-man, MacMurdie. The chief's idea seemed sound to him. But he wanted to verify it a little.

"The Montreal air line runs like so," he said.

He traced a line from Buffalo to Montreal, and noted where it hit the St. Lawrence River. Then he nodded to Benson.

"It runs over the Thousand Islands. That'll be the place. But as ye say, it's a labyrinth. How would we ever get an idea as to what part of the Islands these skurlies'll be hidin' it?"

Benson shook his head a little, pale eyes flaming with concentrated thought.

But it was Smitty, the good-natured looking, moon-faced giant who had an idea first.

"I've got it!" he said so suddenly that MacMurdie jumped and turned resentful blue eyes on the big fellow.

"What have ye got, mon?" he snapped. "The little crawlin' things in your bonnet?"

"You say the plane takes the gang again tonight. And you, sir"—the giant turned to Benson—"have told us how your tragedy and your entrance into this business came from forcing your way into the plane with your wife and child that night. Well, I could perhaps locate their hide-out in the island myself, like this."

He spoke eight words. Benson's eyes seemed to go more colorless than ever, and to become, if possible, brighter. MacMurdie stared open-jawed.

"*Whoosh!*" the Scot said finally. "'Tis suicide, mon! Ye can't do a thing like that!"

"No, Smitty," Benson said. "I can't permit anything like that."

"I could do it," insisted the giant. "That is, I think I could. You!" He stared at MacMurdie. "What plane will they be taking?"

"The S404, of course. The one with the trapdoor."

"You know that plane?"

"Like the inside of my hand."

"Draw the undercarriage. And draw it to scale! Because I'm going to do this—and if your drawing isn't right I'll come back from the grave and haunt you."

"If anything goes wrong ye won't have a grave," said the Scot somberly. "Ye'll be buried in black water in the Ontario."

The Scot was drawing the under carriage of the S404, and being very careful about it.

In Benson's pale and deadly eyes, as they rested on the giant Smitty, was a look not seen there since his hair had whitened and his face died. But he was shaking his head.

"I told you, Smitty, I won't permit it."

The big fellow stared back at him.

"And I'm telling you, sir I'm going to do it. It's the answer, if I can stay alive."

"No!"

"You can't stop me. You downed me once, but you

89

can't do it again. And the only way you can keep me from trying is to get me down and strap me to the floor."

The eyes, pale, but seeming composed of living flame, dwelt on the big fellow's face. There was no seeming stupidity in the moon countenance now. It was vital with intelligence and with resolve. Benson's hand rested on the vast shoulder for just an instant.

"You can have anything I've got, if you pull out of this, Smitty."

"I don't want anything but just to work for you."

Mac passed over his careful drawing.

"Ye're a suicidal fool, Smitty. But ye have your points, you overgrown gorilla. Though, of course, ye haven't a chance in this."

"You're a wet blanket, Scotch," said Smitty, studying the drawing.

And then he was gone, with Benson staring after him with that strange light in his eyes, and MacMurdie's sandy ropes of eyebrows pulled down low.

"I wouldn't tell him to his face," Mac said, "but he's a very brave mon."

Benson only nodded.

"And I wouldn't want to be the man he's after," added the Scot dourly.

The men Smitty was after, and over whom, though they didn't yet realize it, the looming dead face of a man whose soul was as lifeless as his features drew ever closer, were on their way to the Buffalo airport.

That is, four of them were. The four were in an ordinary taxi. They were the big fellow with the black pads of hair on the backs of his hands, who had been a passenger the night Benson went to the men's lavatory, two of the three ordinary-looking men who had also been along, and a newcomer—a dapper, slim man of forty, who was continually smiling with his lips but not with his eyes.

"Rena has the trunk?" the smiling man said.

"Yeah," replied the big fellow with the hairy hands. "The plane is booked solid?"

"You dummy! of course. Think we'd have other passengers?"

"You did, one night, I hear."

The big man snapped out an oath.

"They didn't stay aboard long! And a thing like that can't happen again. We got it fixed so it can't."

The cab dumped them at the airport—four men who were dressed and who acted like any other four businessmen on the verge of a fast trip by plane. Each had a suitcase, of airplane weight. They walked toward the runway.

There, on the flat stretch, a transport stood with idling props. On its nose was painted S402. But it was the S404, all right—the one with the trapdoor. Somebody had decided that the switching of numbers was such a good idea that they'd make it permanent.

The four walked slowly; and in a moment, three other people from another cab caught up to them. There was a light trunk strapped to the back of the cab. The driver and an airport man got the trunk and carried it over the level field to the plane. They stowed it in the tail.

The three from the second cab were two men, average and unremarkable-looking as were the ones in the first taxi, and a woman. The woman was rather pretty, save for a hard line around the mouth. These, too, had innocent-looking airplane luggage with them in addition to the trunk. No one would have any suspicions about them, merely on looking them over. Seven people bound for Montreal by plane. One with a trunk. So what?

They climbed aboard. The props idled a little faster. A third cab drew up at the gate with a scream of brakes. From this cab leaped a figure that looked nine feet tall and five broad.

The giant lit running and raced toward the plane. He was a bizarre figure. For all his size, he had a hump on his back. It made you wonder how tall the tremendous

91

hunchback would have grown if his spine had stayed straight.

"Hold that plane!" he yelled. "I've got to get aboard. Got to get to Montreal in a hurry!"

Aboard, the big fellow with the black pads of hair leaped to the door of the pilot's compartment.

"Get going!" he snapped. "Some fool is trying to get on. Hurry!"

"I can't get away till they take the chocks from under the wheels," said the pilot. He waved wildly to the men on the ground to remove the blocks.

Near the steps still in place up to the plane door, the humpbacked giant who had run from the cab was gesticulating and arguing with a field attendant.

"I don't care if the plane is full! I've got to get aboard. I'll sit in the aisle. And don't try to tell me a ship like this one can't get off the ground with just one passenger over capacity! These boats can take an extra half-ton overload and walk off with it."

The attendant still barred the way. The humpbacked giant simply plucked him up by the collar, held him kicking two feet off the ground in one hand, and then set him aside a yard to the right.

They were closing the plane door. The giant got it, and forced it out against the pull of three men with seeming effortlessness. Then he was inside, beaming good nature and stupidity on the passengers.

"Sorry to cause a disturbance, folks, but I had to get aboard."

The big fellow with the hairy hands was still at the pilot's compartment. The pilot had heard the giant enter.

"Do I stall here till you can throw him off?" he said in a low tone.

"Yes!" the big man answered savagely. Then: "No. Here comes a couple of airport guys not on our payroll. We can't stick around and have a brawl that'll end with the cops sticking their bills in. That flat-faced, over-grown cripple! Well . . . nothing for it but to pull away fast."

The door was slammed and secured. The pilot gave her the gun. The big ship flashed along the runway and majestically rose.

And in one of the seats always so curiously vacant when this crowd booked the plane, sat Smitty, beaming good nature with all his vast face and staring with amiable lack of intelligence at the others.

The pilot said just one word to the man with the black pads of hair.

"Where?"

"Just before we drop the other," snapped the big fellow. "East end of the lake, as soon as you pick up the beacon light in the distance. We'll fix the big dope like we fixed that other dummy who was fool enough to force his way on board. This guy got on at Buffalo— but he'll never get off at Montreal."

CHAPTER XII

Smitty Takes the Risk

A trip in a big transport plane, particularly at night, is not very exciting. The motion is smooth, there is nothing to see out of the windows, and the subdued roar of the motors is lulling. Passengers feel more like dozing than anything else.

The seven in the Montreal plane acted as dull and sleepy as any normal passengers would. Now and then, the big fellow with the hairy hands would lean forward and say something to the man who was always smiling with his lips but not the rest of his face. But that was about the only sign of life any of them gave.

Only the tremendous fellow with the hump on his back seemed excited. He looked as if this were his first plane trip. He stared out the window and down, trying to see something in the June dark, and then grinned at his fellow passengers. He looked like a huge kid with a new red sled. But it wasn't fooling the fellow with the perpetual, meaningless smile.

"I make the guy now," this man said to the big fellow across the aisle from him, voice low enough to be drowned from other ears by the motor hum. "He drove Leon's car."

The big fellow whistled soundlessly.

"So he's not the dope he looks to be! Leon's chauffeur, huh? I suppose he thinks he's disguised, with that hump on his back. Might as well try to disguise Pikes Peak!"

"He must be hired by this Benson guy," said the

smiling man. But his smile was a little worried. "So now what?"

The other shrugged. "You know what. It wouldn't make any difference if he was as harmless as he's tryin' to look. Any way it lays, he goes out the trapdoor just the same."

"He's awful big. And did you see him lift the monkey at the field in one hand?"

"The bigger they are, the harder they fall. Got that stuff in your suitcase?"

"Sure."

"Go and get it."

The smiling man got up, after a moment, and went to the tail of the plane. The stewardess, the same rather pretty girl with the slightly shifty eyes who was always on these runs, got him his bag. The man took from it an innocent-looking handkerchief, and blew his nose loudly. But when he shut the bag, and put the handkerchief in his pocket, there was a small vial of colorless stuff in the linen folds.

The man came back, stared out the window of his side, and then crossed over to Smitty's side. With an apologetic look, he sat in the seat just ahead of Smitty's, and stared out the window there, as though searching for some spot not to be seen from his own seat.

Smitty settled more comfortably against the hump on his back—and waited.

He had told Benson he had an idea how they could find the criminals' headquarters. He had explained in eight words:

"I'll force my way into the plane, too."

Then after he had deliberately placed himself in the position which had spelled such tragedy for his boss, a month ago, Smitty would wait and see what happened. *If* he could out-smart the gang and stay alive!

The first part of the scheme had worked all right. He was aboard the plane, and they were getting close to the Thousand Islands region. But that first part was a cinch compared to the second—staying alive.

Smitty grinned like a pleased kid and watched every move of the others. Particularly he kept his eyes on the man who had just sat in front of him, and who had gone to the rear and gotten a handkerchief from his bag. It was from this source that Smitty expected danger.

Because he was looking ahead so hard, he didn't hear or sense the man *behind* him move a little. This one, a slim, dapper fellow with no chin, stealthily reached to his armpit and got out a gun. He leaned suddenly forward.

Smitty, with all his attention on the man ahead, felt a gun muzzle bore into the back of his neck. He froze. One small move, and he'd have his head nearly blown off. He didn't try to make a move. With one easy maneuver, they had him cold. It might have been expected where the odds were seven to one.

No one said anything. No one moved hastily, now that the huge fellow with the futile hump on his back was caught.

Very leisurely, the smiling man in front of Smitty turned with the handkerchief in his clenched fist. The girl with the hard line around her mouth looked on with wide eyes, but with no protest. The other man just grinned.

The smiling man squeezed hard. The vial in the handkerchief broke, and the sickish smell of chloroform filled the cabin.

"Pilot!" yelled Smitty suddenly. Yelling was all he could do. He could no more disregard the gun at the base of his skull by a physical move than he could fly without wings. "Somebody! Help—"

The chloroform-soaked handkerchief was jammed over his mouth and nose. He did struggle then. But the struggle rapidly grew weaker, then died. The handkerchief was jammed tighter.

The giant slumped in the seat.

Two of the other men were opening the trapdoor. Cool

97

air breezed up from the vacuum formed. They slanted the limp giant toward the oblong.

Two thousand feet below, the ebony-black water of Lake Ontario presented a pavement-hard surface to anything dropped from such a height. Hitting water from there is like hitting granite.

They dropped the big man through. He slid down the backward-slanting door like coal down a chute, and was gone.

The big plane roared steadily on.

The gray fox of a man for whom Smitty had made this supreme sacrifice—in vain, as these killers could have testified—had left the hotel only a few minutes after the giant's departure.

He went to the brokerage firm of Carney & Buell, who handled Buffalo Tap & Die locally and whose New York affiliate had floated the stock issue in the first place. Smitty had said that Leon had had him drive here just before his visit to John Lansing's deserted house.

When the flesh of Benson's countenance had gone dead, it had removed him at a stroke from the world of normal men. But it had done something else, too. It had made him a man of a thousand faces.

A few touches of his steely, sensitive fingers—and he was someone else, with the flesh staying in the place into which it was prodded.

He walked into Carney & Buell's place with his countenance sober and squarish and his hat on the exact center of his head. He was an impressive figure. When he asked to see one of the partners, Wallace Buell came out at once.

"I am Mrs. Martineau's legal adviser," Benson said. "I came to inquire a little about her financial affairs."

Buell's gimlet black eyes widened a little.

"I don't understand. We know Mrs. Martineau, and have had direct dealings with her. But I was not aware that she had retained a legal adviser."

"She hasn't, exactly," Benson said, the perfect picture of a sober, humorless corporation lawyer. "I did work for Robert Martineau before he died. When I read of his widow disposing of her Buffalo Tap & Die stock, which I regard as sound, I decided to investigate a little on my own. Why did she sell that stock, do you suppose, Mr. Buell?"

Buell looked harrassed.

"A dozen people, mainly reporters, have asked me that. Good Heavens, I don't know why! We're only Mrs. Martineau's brokers, not her guardians. Why don't you ask her?"

"I've tried to. I can't get in touch with her." Benson's pale and icy eyes were studying this man, turning him inside out. Was the agitation that of anyone hounded by reporters, or was it caused by fear?

"We have been unable to get in touch with Mrs. Martineau, either," Buell admitted. "Perhaps she has taken a trip without telling anyone. In any event, it's none of our business."

"You won't tell me why she sold?"

"I can't. We got 'sell' orders. That's all I know. And if I did know more, I wouldn't tell you or anybody else," the broker snapped. "I've been questioned too much. Good day to you."

It was about what Benson had expected, but it had been worth making a try, at least, for information from this source.

He went out—to a phone booth, where he dialed a number and placed a handful of change on the phone-booth counter for a long conversation.

Benson, as adventurer, had met thousands of men in positions ranging from that of water-front bum to governors of States. As rich man and business promoter, he had met more thousands, bankers, accountants, stock salesmen. Few men in the world had as varied and prodigious an acquaintanceship as his. He had lines of friendships leading into all sorts of places. And he utilized one of these lines now, as a short cut.

"Carter," he said, when an important voice said "Hello"

after the intervention of a switchboard girl and three secretaries, "this is Dick Benson talking."

The man was Benjamin Carter, vice president of the Buffalo National Bank. He chuckled with delight.

"Dick! You old sawhorse! I didn't know you were in this part of the world. We'll have to get together—"

"Not just now," said Benson. "I called for a little financial information. In rather a hurry—"

"Any financial information I can give *you*, you could put in your eye. You can beat the traders at their own game. But how are things? I heard you got married. Is the wife with you?"

"Yes," said Benson steadily, eyes pale flames. "Yes. I got married. My wife . . . is not with me. I called about the stock of Buffalo Tap & Die, Carter. You probably have the last annual report lying around the bank. Dig it up and give me the dope, will you?"

There was a long pause. Benson dropped coins in the phone box. Carter came back on.

"I got one. Funny thing, though. There was no report in the regular files. I just happened to have this extra one in my desk. Finally remembered about it."

He read down the sheet, and Benson listened with eyes intent but face dead and forever expressionless. Outstanding shares of stock, five hundred thousand, par one hundred. Plant and equipment—current debts—current liabilities—good will—

"Cash reserve on hand, fourteen million two hundred thousand dollars," the banker finished.

"The size of the reserve," said Benson, "puts the firm in a fine, sound spot, I'd say. Why is the stock so low, Carter?"

"It got started down with all the others listed on the board in the current recession," the banker said. "No sense to it, any more than to the drop in other sound stocks. But it has been hammered down even lower by the French leave that seems to have been taken by some of the executives. I'd like to know something about that myself. Everybody in money circles would."

"There's been a lot of the stock dumped at distress prices," said Benson.

"Yes. But no one with sense should sell at the current quotations."

"Mrs. Robert Martineau did."

"Hysterical widow," grunted Carter. "She probably got stampeded into selling by the continual dropping of the stock."

"One more thing," said Benson. "Could you tell me the names of the heaviest stockholders?"

"One of our customers' men was with Carney & Buell for a while," mused Carter. "I think he might know. Just a minute—"

Benson dropped more coins, and then Carter picked it up again:

"There are six, Dick. Lawrence Hickock, Mrs. Martineau, Stephen Vincent, John Lansing, Arnold Leon and Harry Andrews. But why all the curiosity? Have you some stock, too?"

"Just asking around," said Benson expressionlessly.

"You fox! I'll bet you plan to buy a lot low, and wait for a rise. If I had your money—When am I going to see you for a reunion?"

"Soon, I hope," Benson said. "Thanks for the information, Carter. You'll never know how much it has helped."

He hung up. Six principal stockholders. Of the six, four were mysteriously missing—Hickock, Leon, Mrs. Martineau, and Vincent. That left two. A man named Harry Andrews—and John Lansing.

It was to Lansing's home that Leon had been lured, just before his disappearance. It was to Lansing's home that Hickock had gone, after a phone call from there—in spite of the fact that Lansing was supposed to be in Florida at the moment.

Benson called the hotel. MacMurdie's Scotch burr sounded.

"Mac, go to the home of Harry M. Andrews. See if he is there. I have reason to believe he's on our mystery

101

list, so he probably won't be. But check and make sure."

"Right," said MacMurdie. "And then?"

"Report back to the hotel. I'm going there after I make a call myself."

Benson's call was at the Lansing home. Queer how that name had bobbed up so often. Benson had heard the name before ever this sinister mixed-up affair started. He had placed it now.

Lansing owned the Upstate Tool & Machinery Co., a company competing with Buffalo Tap & Die.

At the Lansing house, the repaired door told that the owner had gotten back home. And a moment later, in the vast library of the place, Lansing himself confirmed it.

"Wasn't coming up from Florida all summer. I like the summers down there. But I had to come and see what all this silly business was about. Tap & Die? I own a lot of stock in that—but where do *you* come in on this?"

"You can just call me—a questioner," Benson said evenly.

Lansing, a portly old gentleman with vague brown eyes, stared with a wary gaze.

"Investigator? Private detective?"

"You might call it that," said Benson.

"You're being confounded vague. Why should I answer any of your infernal questions?"

"Because it would look odd if you refused," Benson rapped back. "Some queer things have happened at your house, Mr. Lansing. Are you thinking of selling your Tap & Die stock?"

Something—fear suspicion, alertness, what?—leaped into the man's eyes.

"I may be," he said evasively. "It's down low, and seems to be going lower. No use losing more money than you have to."

"What part of Florida were you in during the past six weeks?"

"West Palm Beach," snapped Lansing. "You can check on that, if you like."

There was a subtle wall going up between him and Benson. The gray-steel man with the pale-gray eyes knew he was done questioning. That is, he could keep on questioning, if he wanted to, but he wouldn't get any more answers. At least, he had found out one thing.

Here was *one*, at least, of Tap & Die's big stockholders who had not mysteriously vanished.

He went back to his hotel. At the entrance, an enterprising newsie was crying the latest edition. And this time a financial item had strayed from the rear of the paper to a small box on the front page.

Buffalo Tap & Die had dropped in the face of an otherwise rising market. Another large block of stock had been sold on the decline. It was rumored that Mr. John Lansing, just home from a sojourn in Florida, had sold.

Benson's pale eyes glittered. Lansing had already disposed of his stock, at the very moment when he was telling him that he "might sell."

The gray fox of a man went up to the suite—and the phone was ringing. A voice, in a whisper, greeted him.

"Thank Heaven, ye're there."

"Mac!" said Benson. "What's wrong? Why are you talking so low? I can hardly hear you."

"Trouble, mon," whispered the Scot, over the miles of wire. "They've got me. Andrews'—"

The line went dead, after Benson had heard a sort of gasp—and then a moan.

CHAPTER XIII

The Clue

Andrews' home was modest for a man of his means. It was a large shingle bungalow at the dead end of a residence street, and cost a third of the sums that must have been spent on the other big homes around. It had extensive grounds, though, and was hidden from the road by shrubbery.

Benson glided among the bushes and trees in his silent, jaguar fashion. Mac in there—in desperate trouble of some sort!

At a glance, the house seemed to be vacant. All the shades were down against the dying sun. Not a soul could be seen—

But then Benson did see someone, and his pale, deadly eyes narrowed. A man had stepped furtively from around a corner of the house. The sly look of him, and the way he kept glancing around, told he was a guard—and a crook. Something was going on in that house which was not supposed to be interrupted.

Benson got out Mike, the unique, specially designed little revolver. He took the half-second aim of the sure marksman. There was a soft *spat* as Mike spoke in his usual silenced whisper.

And the man dropped, out for at least an hour.

Benson stole to the house and around to the rear. There was a heavy, blank door. He tried the knob, softly, and the door opened a fraction of an inch.

Benson paused there, hand on the knob, face as dead as a mask of white wax, but eyes flaming like ice in a colorless sun. Whoever was inside seemed to have placed a great deal of confidence in the guard, to leave the door unlocked. Or else the man had just stepped out for a look around and had not bothered to lock the door for the short time he meant to be out.

Benson went in. He made absolutely no sound as he went across the bare kitchen floor. You'd have thought he wasn't quite touching the boards, but was floating an inch above them. He got to a swinging door and, after listening, went through that.

He entered the room fast, for on first opening the door he had gotten a glimpse of a chair leg—with a man's leg roped to it!

He was in a dining room. The table had been pushed against a far wall, leaving most of the room clear. In the center of it was a chair. And to it was roped Mac-Murdie.

The Scot was bound at arms and legs and waist to the heavy chair. He was gagged. At the sides of the cloth that went around his head to keep the gag in place, his large red ears stuck out like distress signals. Over the gag his frosty blue eyes blazed.

But there was more in them than fury or fear. There was in them some kind of terribly urgent message.

Benson stepped toward him—and two doors opened.

From one, at the side hall, came two men. From the other, opening into a front room, another stepped. And then, from the swing door he had just entered, a fourth appeared.

Each of the four had a gun. And in the eyes of each was murder. The whole thing had been a trap, and a devilishly perfect one.

Benson stood stone-still. To have done otherwise, with four guns pointing at his body at close range, would have been silly. But his eyes were pale flame; and each of the four gunmen, meeting that pallid, deadly glance, felt something like a shock strike him.

MacMurdie's face—what you could see of it for the

gag—was one bony, red picture of contrition at having got Benson into this jam. But Benson didn't stare at it long. He looked at the four killers.

They closed in even more on him.

"Go over him," said one, the tallest.

One of the other three stepped to Benson, and around him. Coming up warily from the back, so Benson couldn't possibly grab him and use him as a shield, he ran his hands over Benson's body from neck to knees.

"No rod," he said, "The guy's a sap."

The tall man jerked his head to another of the dining-room chairs. There were two in the set of eight that had arms. Mac sat in one. Benson was to sit in the other.

He sat down. Again, it would have been crazy not to. And Benson didn't do crazy things. From behind a rope was looped around his body, and he was all through.

They tied him at wrists and ankles and waist to the chair, as MacMurdie was tied. The Scots eyes were terrible in their fury and self-reproach as he watched. One of the killers grinned and leveled his gun.

The tall man knocked his arm aside.

"You dummy! If somebody found a slug in one of 'em, the whole show would be off."

So they didn't shoot the gray man with the white face that, even at such a moment, did not move a muscle. And that was their mistake.

"Scatter around, you guys. You know what to do."

The men left, swiftly, going out different doors. Each door was bolted as they went. Benson and the Scot could possibly move around a little, taking the chairs with them, but that, the gang thought, wouldn't do any good with the doors locked.

And that was another mistake.

The moment they were alone, Benson began shoving his chair. With his ankles tied to the chair legs, he could only move the chair by pushing, a little at a time, with the tips of his toes. It was like trying to push an automobile only with the tips of your fingers. But Benson had steel cables for muscles. The calves of his legs rippled—and the chair moved along the floor.

He got to MacMurdie and edged around so that his left side was at the Scot's right. Then he tipped back in his chair. Not just a little—all the way back.

The chair banged to the floor and left him with his head down and his legs up. His left leg, strapped to the chair leg, was almost parallel with MacMurdie's right arm, strapped to the arm of the chair.

One of the doors opened in a hurry as a man, drawn by the sound of the falling chair, poked his head in to be sure everything was all right. The man grinned murderously at Benson's helpless, upside-down position, and went out again.

But if Benson's position was helpless at the moment, it was designed to bring help swiftly. And the quick-witted Scot caught on at once.

MacMurdie could move his hand only a little, what with the rope around his wrist. But he could move it enough to inch Benson's trousers leg up over his calf—and get at Ike, the razorlike throwing dagger, at the bulge of Benson's leg.

He slashed the rope at Benson's left ankle; then, as Benson whirled the chair around with his free leg, cut the rope at his right. Legs untied, by a miracle of co-ordination, Benson tipped upright again, chair and all.

They were free in half a minute after that.

"Mon, I'm so sorry I dragged ye here," Mac whispered, when his gag was off. "They caught me. I got loose for a minute and got to a phone. I didn't realize 'twas just what they wanted—for me to call you."

"Forget it, Mac," Benson said. "We'd better get out the window—"

The swinging door from the kitchen flew open. A man stood on the threshold, startled eyes lining on Benson's chest over the sights of an automatic. Behind the man something blue and misty curled up in the kitchen.

Benson's arm came forward with seemingly no back-swing as a preliminary at all. Ike flew from his whipping hand. The slim, deadly needle of steel with the light, hollow handle, streaked almost as fast as a bullet toward the man in the doorway.

The man had been squeezing the trigger. He tried to shoot and side-step, too, and accomplished nothing constructive in either direction. His shot missed the man with the white, dead face, and his body did not miss Ike. The knife ended its whispering flight in the fleshy part of the man's right arm.

"Pete—" the man yelled.

MacMurdie's mallet-like, bony fist got him then. The Scot knocked him cold, but the harm was done. There were running steps.

No time for the window, now. Benson and MacMurdie backed up to a door apiece, so that the swinging panels would hide their bodies, and waited. And as they waited they smelled smoke and heard the ominous crackle of flames licking at dry wood.

They didn't wait long. The other three men were in the room in answer to the cry for help in only a few seconds. All came in the door behind which Benson lurked.

The tall man snapped his gun up to kill the Scot. Benson's flashing toe cracked his wrist and sent the gun flying. Another shot at MacMurdie, too hastily, and whirled to shoot Benson down. He went down himself, with a broken jaw. The third man ran.

"Get him!"

MacMurdie didn't need the command. The Scot's bony figure was flying after the fellow. His huge feet were eating up the hallway three yards to the gunman's one. He got him at the front door. The man went down—and stayed down.

And then it was time to get out of there.

In four different places, the gang had set the Andrews house afire. The house, of wood throughout with a shingled exterior, would go up in twenty minutes or less, razed to the foundations. To speed the fire, gasoline had been used. That was why the men hadn't shot Mac-Murdie or Benson. The two were supposed to have been consumed untraceably in the flames. But their bodies might be found, and bullets in them would have tipped the show that the deaths were murder and not accidental, due to fire.

"Out!" snapped Mac, fumbling with the front door.

"These men, Mac!"

On the Scot's face was a terrible look. He stared at the nearest flames, and he thought of his drugstore, bombed with his wife and boy in it. Then he thought of the trip to the undertaker for wife and son.

"Let 'em burn!" he rasped. "Death's too good for rats like these!"

"But death by fire, Mac—"

"It's still too good for 'em. Come on out!"

Benson caught the Scot's furious arm.

"Come along. We'll carry them out."

"I'll na' have naught to do wi' the skurlies!" swore the Scot, burr broadening with the stress of the moment.

But in the flaming gray eyes of Benson was command. And in a moment MacMurdie shrugged.

"Ye're a fool, mon! They'd have done for ye. Now 'tis providence that their own fire should do for them."

They carried the four out. Down the street a fire siren screamed. Benson laid the four on the lawn and went through their pockets, hands moving so fast they seemed two pale blurs.

There was only one thing he bothered to take from any of them; only one thing of significance. That was a postcard. There was a picture of blue water and an impossibly beautiful island on the card. On the other side, under special-delivery stamp, which is a rarity on a postcard, were two words:

Insulin. Fast.

It was signed "Murdock."

The two left. As the fire engines drew up before the Andrews home, which was too far gone already to be saved, Benson and MacMurdie were speeding toward the hotel in the fast roadster.

There Benson picked up the telephone. As he used it, he stared at the postcard. The picture was of some island called Farquer's Knob. But the postmark was Isle Royale.

Benson called Mrs. Martineau's home and got the name of her regular physician. Then he called the physician. He repeated the process with Andrews, Vincent and Hickock. And there he stopped and stared at Mac.

"Got it," he said. "Lawrence Hickock suffers from diabetes—has to have insulin."

He looked again at the card.

"Hickock, a prisoner of this gang, must have insulin or die. So they've sent for some. Sent the message from Isle Royale, which is near Kingston, Canada, in the Thousand Island district. The hide-out will be near there Mac. This clue is going to do the trick, I think. And we'd never have gotten it if we hadn't dragged those rats out of the fire they richly deserved to die in. Virtue sometimes *is* its own reward."

CHAPTER XIV

Isle Royale

On the Buffalo-Montreal plane, from which Smitty had been dropped with nothing but two thousand feet of air beneath him and the dark lake, there was scurrying activity. The man with the black pads of hair on his knuckles had seen, far ahead, a tiny pinpoint of light.

That light was the beacon pointing to the gang's secret lair.

"O.K.," he grunted.

The man with the perpetual, greasy smile, and another, went to the trunk in the tail. They opened it. The bound, gagged figure of a man showed in the trunk. But the man needn't have been gagged. He was elderly, frail-looking, and was mercifully unconscious. It was Arnold Leon.

They lifted Leon from the trunk, and put a cork life preserver around his spare shoulders.

"Hurry it! Almost there!" called the pilot through the open front-compartment door, over the motors' drone.

Hastily they strapped a parachute over Leon's body. They carried him back to the trapdoor, which two other men already had open.

"Now!" called the pilot. The pinpoint of light was directly underneath.

They let the unconscious man slide down the chute formed by the slanting door.

"Hope that parachute opens all right," said the man with the meaningless smile uneasily.

"They've always opened before. I guess this one will now."

It had opened as they spoke, though, already far astern, it couldn't be seen. Leon was dropping toward the surface of Lake Ontario, far below.

And after the huge white mushroom from which dangled Arnold Leon, another, darker shape was plummeting!

Smitty, when he had asked MacMurdie to draw the undercarriage of the S404 strictly to scale, had laid his desperate plan on one thing—the forward-slanting brace of the rear wheel making a tricycle landing gear for the plane. That brace, he believed, could be reached from the rear end of the trapdoor.

He had held his breath when the chloroform was jammed to mouth and nose. But even at that, he had gotten enough of the stuff at the end, when he couldn't hold on any longer, to fog his brain with beginning unconsciousness.

The deadly slide down the door, however, had cleared his brain again. He was sliding, feet first, on his side. He cleared the door—and whirled.

The plane, traveling better than two hundred feet a second, whipped overhead the instant the air resistance slowed his own initial momentum. But even at that, Smitty caught the rear wheel brace by little more than the tips of his fingers. The screaming gale promptly snapped him back so that he trailed almost straight out like a pennant. But then he had his enormous hands squarely on the brace; and when those hands caught hold of something, they held.

He hung there, great muscles quivering with the strain, till he got over his sick feeling. One thing to plan a try like this—another entirely when it came to putting it into operation! Then he performed the appalling feat of hanging by one great hand while with the other he tore off his coat and a mass of padding in the back.

He shifted hands, and got the coat off over the other

114

sleeve. On his back was revealed a compact parachute. That, plus padding to hide the outlines, was the "hump" on his back. The hump had been only incidentally for a disguise.

He saw the trapdoor come down again. From his place up almost against the belly of the transport, he could not see in the door any more than those inside could see him on the outside. But in a moment he saw a bound body slide through.

The man dropped, and a white cloud of canvas billowed out and broke the fall. Smitty instantly dropped, too, and plummeted down after the white cloud.

"Whew!" he said, shaken and beaded with cold sweat. If ever a guy had looked Death squarely in the eyes—and spat in his face—

He rocked in the swing of his own parachute. This chute was not white. It was black. It blended against the sky so well that only by a blotting out of stars could an observer from below spot it. And there were no stars tonight. A June rain was brewing, and the sky was lowering and black.

A parachute seems to float slowly but it actually falls all too fast. In a very short time the white parachute settled to one side of an unconscious elderly man who splashed deep and then bobbed up on the cork preserver.

Smitty, feet first, to minimize his own splash as much as possible, hit an instant later. He writhed from the 'chute cords at his vast shoulders.

The sound of a motorboat throbbed. It came swiftly toward the spot.

"There's the 'chute—that white blot," a man said, from the boat. "Hit it fast Murdock. We want him alive, at least for a little while."

Smitty swam soundlessly in the ebony water till the boat, from the engine noise, was directly in front of him on a line with the unconscious man. He could see the floating body. In a few minutes he saw the boat, too—without lights, and only a black hulk against black sky and water. There was a grinding sound as the motor was reversed, bringing the boat neatly to a stop alongside the body.

"Up with him!"

From the high side of the boat, a fairly sizeable motor cruiser, a boathook dipped down. It caught under the strap of the life preserver, was raised, lifted, preserver and body and all.

"Out cold, but still breathin'. Guess he'll be all right—for as long as we want him," said the unseen man on the cruiser's dark deck.

The boat started off, lightless into the darkness of Lake Ontario in the labyrinth of the Thousand Islands region. But there was one more passenger aboard than the skipper reckoned.

Out of the black lake, as the boat halted, two huge arms had reached up. Great hands caught the flukes of the anchor, at the bow. And the hands were followed by a giant's body as the boat shot forward.

Smitty lay in darkness at the bow, while the motor cruiser went at thirty miles an hour toward the core of the mystery which Benson was scheming like a gray fox to solve—

Isle Royale.

The name was bombastic; the island didn't carry out the royal promise. It was small, had a dozen log shacks on it which a few resorters had rented. There was a general store, which was also the post office. That was all. There was no phone, because no one had bothered to meet the expense of laying a phone cable underwater to mainland. For the same reason, there was no telegraph.

That was why the post card had been sent asking for insulin. There was no way to get word out except by mail.

Into the general store, at nine next morning, a man

strode with a lithe, jaguar tread. He had just come by hired motorboat after a trip by chartered plane.

The man had snow-white hair, though the latent power in his movements, and the skin of hands and neck, told that he was in his thirties. His face was as expressionless as a sack of flour. But his eyes were not expressionless. They were coldly flaming, almost colorless gray. Eyes of ice; eyes seemingly designed for the sole purpose of peering at enemies over gun sights.

Hair white, eyes light gray, clothes darker gray. All gray. He was like a limber steel bar, rather than a man.

Down at the rickety dock that serviced Isle Royale, behind a pile of crates, was a tall, bony man with a map of Scotland written on his face. Hands like knobby mallets were jammed into his pockets. His ears stood out like sails. But there was nothing amusing about his eyes—cold and bitterly blue.

The two were on the trail of that post card. A man named Murdock had written for insulin. Presumably the man would call for the insulin with the first mail, which came by boat to Isle Royale at nine to nine thirty a.m.

Benson was at the general store and post office to see who asked for a package in the name of Murdock.

MacMurdie was at the dock to see who landed and keep tabs on them.

Benson, gray eyes narrowed to hide their pale flame, asked for a package of cigarettes. The storekeeper, a little sparrow of a man with a ragged brown mustache, dug them out of a fly-specked case.

"Goin' to stay here a spell?" chirped the storekeeper. "I got a mighty nice cabin for rent, if you are."

"I may," said Benson. "Some friends are to come late this afternoon. I came on ahead to see if we'd like to put up here for a while. Rather chilly, it seems to me."

"It's still June," said the storekeeper. "Up here we don't get hot weather till about the first of July. Then it's hot enough. But my cabin has a fireplace in it—"

Benson let the man ramble on. As he waited, he looked

117

out the dusty front window. In a few minutes he saw a man coming toward the store from the direction of the dock. The man was big and shambling, in old pants and a sweater. He walked with his arms held crooked at his side like an ex-wrestler.

"I wonder if I could have a drink of water?" Benson said.

"Sure, sure," said the storekeeper. "Right through the door to the back. I live back there. You'll find water in the icebox, nice and cold."

Benson went back, leaving the door open a crack. The big man in old pants and sweater came in.

"Mornin'," Benson heard the storekeeper chirp. "How's *your* little old island this mornin'? Or don't you live on an island?"

The man grunted something unintelligible.

"What say?" the storekeeper asked. "Mainland?"

"I didn't say," the man growled back. "Got a package for me?"

"There's a package for a Mr. Murdock. It's small but kind of heavy and marked fragile. Special delivery." The storekeeper chuckled. "I guess them city folks in Buffalo didn't know special delivery don't mean anything when you got to haul mail fourteen miles by boat."

"Gimme it," said the man. There was a pause. Then, in a slightly different voice, he said: "Got to get some things. Pack 'em up as I read from this list."

He ordered a good deal of stuff. So much that the storekeeper said in a pleased tone: "Must be quite a passel of you at wherever you're stayin'. Camp?"

"No not a camp. Just some friends," the man growled impatiently.

Back in the rear room, Benson was leaning against the wall and shaking as though he'd just had a chill.

The man named Murdock! The package with insulin, indicating surely that Lawrence Hickock, one of the victims, was on the other end of the route traveled by this man! And now—provisions for many people!

It was the end of the hunt. Only a few miles away

118

was the hide-out of this gang of murderers into whose grip he had blundered that night in Buffalo when he forced his way aboard the plane.

Groceries for many people! Were his wife and girl among those people only a few short miles from here? It was this thought that had completely unstrung Benson, the man of gray metal and cold flame, for the moment. He could see, behind his closed and quivering eyelids, Alicia's face. The soft brown eyes in it seemed to be imploring him to come to her rescue swiftly. And beside her was little Alice.

Were they alive? Were they near him now?

All his common sense told him they were dead. But for the moment he had to dismiss common sense, or go mad.

The man, Murdock, was padding out of the store. Benson rallied all his iron will and composed himself. Calm again but with sweat-drenched face, he came back into the store.

"Get your water?" nodded the storekeeper. "That's fine. Goin' for a stroll around the island? You'll find it ain't very big. Keep that cabin of mine in mind if you want to rent—"

Benson thanked him and went out. He walked casually in the opposite direction taken by Murdock—till he had got out of the storekeeper's range of vision through the front window. Then he darted to the right, circled the store building, and headed toward the dock.

It was broad daylight. The absence of people in the small cluster of houses around the store made any moving thing conspicuous. But Benson had long ago learned to move quite inconspicuously, even under such conditions.

A tree here. A clump of bushes there. A closed and boarded hot-dog stand a little farther on. A pile of crates—

Benson got to the pile of crates alongside the docks at the moment Murdock reached a fast motor cruiser

119

moored there. It was about thirty feet from crates to boat. Benson crouched on the balls of his feet. Murdock began stowing provisions into the rear cockpit of the boat.

Benson silently walked toward the man. Murdock had his back turned. Again Benson seemed to drift, like a gray wraith, an inch above the ground rather than on it, so soundless was his tread.

Murdock bent to lift the rope from the cleat in the dock and cast off. Benson sprang.

And his foot slipped at last.

There was a little rasping sound of leather on wood, and Murdock whirled with a rapping oath to see the gray man leaping at him. As fast as Benson had ever seen it done. Murdock had a gun whipped out and pointing. Benson stopped, less than a yard from Murdock, with the gun boring at his chest.

"A dick, eh?" snarled Murdock. In his flat face was a blend of murderous fury and colossal fear. "So somebody's tumbled at last. But you've only got as far as Isle Royale. And nobody could guess the place even from here."

Benson wondered where MacMurdie was. A little chill touched him. He wondered if this man, so alert, so fast on the draw, had caught the Scotchman off base and slugged him. Or, perhaps, hit hard enough to—kill him.

"Get into the boat—and keep a yard away from me while you do it!" Murdock snarled.

Benson moved slowly, looking toward the tiny village. But there would be no help from that direction. The pile of crates chanced to cut off the boat from sight of anyone on the dirt road the village called a street.

Benson got into the boat. Still no sign of MacMurdie.

"Up forward, in the cabin," said Murdock. "And keep your back toward me!"

The boat was an expensive model. There was a starter, with the other controls in the rear cockpit. It whirred as Murdock's hand touched the button. The engine purred into life, and the boat slid out.

"Smart guy, eh?" Murdock's voice came over the subdued roar of the motor, now running smoothly and at high speed as the boat shot forward into the lake. "We'll see how smart you are in a thousand feet of water. We'll see if you can think your way out of it when I put a lump on your knob and drop you over the side, six or seven miles out. You'll never report whatever you've found out. And by the time others pick up your trail, we'll all be through and gone."

The boat sliced at thirty miles an hour through the water; the same boat that without its skipper knowing it, had borne the giant Smitty over the same surface the night before.

CHAPTER XV

Island Prisoners

Smitty had found himself in a very hot spot after he'd succeeded in hauling himself up on this motor cruiser's foredeck.

Black water. Black sky. Pitch darkness all around, and the boat was running without lights. But even this scarcely served to conceal the giant.

The boat, a thirty-footer, had eight feet of high foredeck; then fifteen feet of trim cabin; then rear, open cockpit. The foredeck was only two feet below the top of the cabin. Windows in the front of the cabin, raked the strip of deck.

The unseen two who were controlling the boat were running her from the open rear cockpit, but all they had to do was look hard through the cabin hatchway, through the front strip of glass—and see the giant dark form huddling next to the rail on the deck. It seemed to Smitty that if either so much as lit a cigarette, the glow from the butt would reveal him.

However, neither lit a cigarette. The run was too short.

Smitty had not been in his cramped and perilous position for more than five or six minutes when he sensed more than saw a bulk of land ahead and heard the motor cut to lower speed. They'd timed the dropping of their victims well, with the beacon light square underneath. Less than a mile had intervened between the spot and the place where the unconscious elderly man had splashed into the water.

123

"This it?" said one of the men in the dark cockpit.

"Yeah," was the reply, in a more authoritative voice.

"Nice dark spot."

"It's got things to help besides darkness, as you'll find out after you've been here awhile."

The motor was idling, now, and the boat was drifting. Smitty restrained a cry of surprise. The drift was squarely toward the black, sheer face of a low cliff. It was a solid wall of rock against which the boat must surely ram hard enough, even at this speed, to open her seams.

Light glared out suddenly from the top of the rock wall. Blinding, after the sudden darkness, it bathed the boat.

"O.K.," said a voice by the light. "Just wanted to check and be sure it was you—Hey! Who's that on the foredeck?"

Smitty moved as if he were a hundred-pound stripling instead of weighing nearly three hundred. He writhed sideways, and had his vast bulk over the low rail so fast that it seemed a mere sliding shadow.

As he dropped to the water, his face was bleak with fury and defeat. To have come this far—actually to the core of the mystery itself—and be discovered!

He sank, meaning to swim underwater and away from the boat. But the water was less than five feet deep. At that depth the searchlight could penetrate the water and impale him like a fly on a pin. He charged for the rear of the boat to get behind it. A boat hook shot down and caught him by the belt. It stopped his rush through the clogging water. He whirled, gave one vicious yank on the pole, and saw a form fall headfirst into the water. He started on.

Another boathook shot down toward him. But this did not reach to catch him. It spanged against the side of his head like an iron-tipped lance. And that was all Smitty knew for a while.

Voices, heard dimly and seemingly from a far distance, came finally to Smitty's ears. He heard them as though in a dream as he slowly came to his senses.

"We ought to have killed the big gorilla."

"Orders," another said. "Farr wants to have a talk with the guy before we put the skids to him. Who is he, anyhow? And how did he get here, at this time of night, at the same time as the old guy they dropped from the plane?"

"Yeah, it's kind of funny," a third voice agreed.

"Kind of funny! Is that all you can call it? Here this guy drops in on us. And there's no boat around, no other plane but the transport's been over, and we're too far from anywhere to swim. How'd he get here? It's the answer to questions like those that Farr wants before we snuff him out. Besides, Farr wants to know if any more guys are around."

"Maybe the big fella won't talk."

"He'll talk." The voice was very grim. "You ain't seen what Farr can do when he really wants answers!"

There was silence. Smitty realized that he was bobbing up and down—being carried. And he had heard three panting voices. It took three men to drag his vast bulk.

He heard hollow steps as he was carried onto a wooden porch, then the bang of a door. He fought to get his strength back, but couldn't. The sock on the head had been too severe.

He was carried down steps, and there was a clammy, underground feel to the air.

"I don't like all this," one of his bearers said uneasily. "I ain't yellow. You both know that. But I don't like the smell of this wholesale snatching. All these folks, big shots and a couple bump-offs thrown in, and maybe more to come—I don't like it!"

"Don't be a sap!" panted one of the others. "Know what we split on this? A million fish! Roll that under your tongue. One million dollars, twelve ways! And no telling what the guys higher up will take. This is *big*. Worth takin' a few chances for."

Smitty heard another door open and stirred feebly.

"Hurry it up!" snapped one of the men. "The guy's

waking up. And I don't want to be around when he does —if he's still loose!"

Smitty was dumped to a cold concrete floor. He heard a woman's suppressed scream, and the sound of more men's voices. He opened his eyes. Pain from the lump on his head blurred everything. He shut his eyes again.

Cold metal clamped on wrists and ankles. Then one of the men laughed, and he heard three sets of footfalls as they went away, and the slam of a door.

But still after these three had gone, he heard the frightened babble of men's voices.

Smitty had come very close to concussion of the brain with that vicious jab of the boat hook. Over half an hour more passed before he had even a shadow of his normal strength. Then, when he could open his eyes without having the light hit them like sharp knives, he looked around.

He was in the large basement of what seemed a standard, though old, house. There was a rusted furnace in the center. The light was subdued, because the only illumination was a single small electric bulb, near the furnace. The light showed two small basement windows, heavily barred.

There were five people in the basement besides himself —four men and a woman.

Of the four men he recognized his former employer, lying white and still on the floor. Over him bent a burly man with graying hair and iron-gray burnsides whom Smitty faintly recognized after a while as an acquaintance of his ex-boss, Lawrence Hickock, nicknamed Old Ironsides.

The other two men, though Smitty did not know them by sight, were Stephen Vincent and Harry Andrews.

Hickock shook his leonine head.

"They're animals—not men!" he growled. "Leon is apt to die, without attention. But they don't care—if they get his signature first. The murderers!"

At a little distance, the woman coughed and shivered as she stared, white-faced, at the still-unconscious Leon.

"And there's Mrs. Martineau," said Hickock savagely. "Apt to get pneumonia from being held in this cold, damp cellar. But do these men care? No. They've got what they want from her. Let her die."

Vincent spoke up, lips a thin, firm line in his harried face.

"That's why I'm refusing to sign," he snapped. "I will not allow brutes like them to get away with it!"

Hickock stared at him moodily.

"There's a time for heroics," he said, "but this isn't one of them. They've got us. Might as well face that fact. I'd rather lose some money—a lot of money—than my life. And I think you would, too, when you think it over a little more logically."

"No man with a spark of courage—"

"Oh, don't be a fool!" snapped Hickock. Evidently the imprisonment here had worn nerves and tempers raw. "Look at Mrs. Martineau. A few days more in this hole may kill her. Look at the rest of us. At the mercy of these yapping dogs. If just one refuses what they want, we may all die. Can't you understand that? It took me about two hours to get over my noble courage. Then I signed. If you have sense, you'll do it, too."

Vincent chewed at his lips. "Maybe you're right."

Smitty had found that he was lying right against a wall. He tried to get up now, and heard chains jangle and felt himself jerked to one side.

He was chained to the stone wall of the basement. The men were taking no chances with his great size and strength. Iron bands were around wrists and ankles, with lengths of chain the size of the cross links on tire chains going from the bands to iron loops sunk in the stonework.

The woman and Hickock and Andrews and Vincent stared at the sound of the chain links.

"Who are you?" said Andrews. "Do you own stock in Tap & Die, too?"

Smitty shook his head—and wished that he hadn't. The pain was still enough to be sickening.

"Are you out to rescue us, then? Are there others near?" said Hickock eagerly.

"I came alone," said Smitty.

Hickock sighed. And the four relapsed into apathy. On the floor, Leon stirred a little and moaned.

Smitty looked around more carefully, in the hope that he would see a woman with tawny-gold hair and soft-brown eyes, and a little girl. But if his chief's wife and child were here, at least they were not in this part of the house.

Smitty began rubbing his manacled wrists, behind him, against the rough cement wall. Rubbing, rubbing, with the others not even bothering to look. Mrs. Martineau, forty and frail-looking, coughed with a premonition of deathly illness soon to come if medical attendance weren't provided quickly.

The slow night passed. Daylight swelled through the heavily barred basement windows. Smitty rubbed his chains against the wall behind him.

CHAPTER XVI

Quick-Change Artist

The ten o'clock sun, which could only with difficulty get into two heavily barred basement windows, was brilliant on the glittering surface of Lake Ontario.

In the seeming center of the brilliance, floated a fast motor cruiser, engine cut off and idling.

Far in the distance on every hand, vague smudges showed on the horizon. Islands of varying sizes in this honeycomb of submerged hilltops. Straight ahead was the nearest island—perhaps four miles off.

In the cabin of the cruiser, standing with his face to the bow, Benson waited for developments, pale eyes flaming, steely muscles tense.

Murdock, sitting behind him in the cockpit, with gun trained through the broad opening of the cabin hatchway on his back, had said he was to be dropped overside in a thousand feet of water. Very well. But if he were just dropped, he would float. Benson didn't think Murdock would want a floating body around, apt to be discovered.

It was dollars to doughnuts that the man meant to weight him down, somehow, before dropping him over the side. To do that, Benson thought, he'd have to come close. And if he came close—Benson was going to get him, gun or no gun.

Benson, though Murdock didn't even dream it, was on that boat of his own volition. Murdock's attention had been drawn to him on the dock when Benson's foot slipped.

But Benson's foot had slipped on purpose. The gray jaguar of a man was too sure-footed ever to have made that noise by accident. He had wanted to be "captured" in the hope that Murdock would take him to the hideout of the gang.

Well, he'd been captured. But he wasn't going to the hideout. He was going to a watery death, unless he could overpower Murdock when the man drew near to tie a weight to him.

But with the boat drifting and ready, Murdock said: "Keep on standing right where you are, dummy. I'd just as soon put a slug in you as not!"

Then Murdock moved around. Benson heard him. And in the clear glass of the cabin windows before him, the gray man could catch a faint reflection of action behind him.

Murdock was taking a smaller, spare anchor from the side locker whose lid made one of the cockpit seats. From the same locker he drew a coil of half-inch rope.

"Like fish?" Murdock taunted. "They'll be your buddies in a minute—for a long time."

Benson, experimentally, turned a little. Like light the man had dropped the rope and had his gun in his right hand. Benson stooped over a little. If he could get Mike out of his right leg holster, or Ike out of the left—

"Straighten up!" snapped Murdock, jabbing the gun forward. "I'm taking no chances with you."

Benson straightened. He knew Murdock would prefer not to shoot, because sound carries so far and so clearly over water. But he knew the man *would* shoot, if he felt it necessary. He could always say later he'd shot at a floating bottle or what not.

Benson would have to abide by his first idea—get Murdock when he drew near to fasten the weight to him.

But that plan didn't pan out, either. Murdock was an old hand. He made a loop of the end of the rope, and came to the hatchway.

From a distance of six or seven feet, far too great for Benson to get at him swiftly, he tossed the loop with his right hand, holding the gun ready in his left.

The loop settled over Benson's body. Murdock yanked it taut. The loop held Benson's arm at his sides. Only then, chuckling evilly, did Murdock come close, gun lax.

"Going to jump me, huh?" he said. "Well, bigger men than you have tried to—"

His voice broke in a wild scream. Benson's arms were held to his sides, but he could move his hands—and he had!

Steel fingers gripped over Murdock's legs just above the knees. Like iron claws they bit and twisted, and the punishment of it was testified by Murdock's hoarse yells.

Murdock came out of his fog of agony enough to remember that he had a gun. He leaned back away from Benson to get clear and use it.

Benson had been waiting for the move. He shoved backward, hard. The shove, plus the backward leaning, sent Murdock flying backward to fall in a heap in the center of the little cabin. His head banged the deck.

Foggily he raised his gun. But Benson, arms swelling loose from the slip-noose, was on him before he could shoot. He got the gun with one powerful swoop. Murdock cried out again as he stared into pale and deadly eyes flaming from a white, still face that in the midst of turmoil showed no emotion whatever.

Then Benson swung the gun.

There was silence, broken by a thump from the cockpit. Benson leveled the gun. The thump had come from the locker across from the one in which Murdock had found rope and spare anchor.

"Come out of there, or I'll shoot!"

The lid opened. A red, raw face showed, at each side of which was an outstanding red ear, like a sail. Frosty blue eyes stared into Benson's deadly gray ones.

"MacMurdie!"

"I'd have got the skurlie with a boat hook, if you hadn't nabbed him," MacMurdie said calmly enough.

"Mac! How—"

"I saw the man come in this boat, from behind the crates. I saw him go into the general store, and twigged he was Murdock. So I changed our plans, I hid in the locker, thinkin' the boat would bear me to where we want to go, and that later I could get back and lead ye to it. But it seems ye came along, too."

Already circumstances had proved what a rare man this red-faced, bony-fisted Scot with the enormous feet was. This capped it.

Benson's hand touched the bony shoulder for an instant.

"Thanks," he said. Then, voice expressionless again as his dead, white face: "But the plan has misfired. We didn't find where the hideout is—"

"I'm thinkin' we did," MacMurdie interrupted. He went back to the locker in which he'd hidden, bent down, and came up with a dirty, water-stained piece of paper.

"It seems more than one mon runs this boat. So for the convenience of those who might not know the lake around here to the last detail, some laddie among the gang we're after drew a neat little chart. And here it is. I found it when I jumped into that fish-smelling coffin."

Benson spread it out. Rough pencil lines showed an island with a curiously shaped tree on a high point. The tree was low on one side and high on the other. It resembled a gigantic setting hen.

In a line from the east to the tree, the shore was indicated as a straight low cliff. And in the cliff was a black circle, arching from the water.

"A hole in the cliff!" said Benson, pale eyes blazing. "That's their dock!"

MacMurdie nodded. The meaning was plain.

"And that's our island dead ahead," added Benson.

Even from that distance the two could see the tree resembling a setting hen.

Benson slid the clutch, and the motor started bearing the motor cruiser toward the island.

"Mon, mon!" expostulated MacMurdie. " 'Tis broad

daylight. We haven't a chance of landing on that island, with no guessin' how many of the murderous rats waiting to greet us. We ought to wait till night—"

"We go now," said Benson. There was death in the pale eyes. "My . . . wife and daughter . . . may be on that island, Mac. And every passing hour might make it too late."

"But the minute one of the skurlies sees us, the game is over," said MacMurdie earnestly.

"I think not," said Benson. "Bring Murdock into the light."

Benson dug around and found a half of a cracked mirror. He propped Murdock on the floor, back against the wall, and sat beside the still-unconscious man. Mac held the mirror so that both faces, side by side, were reflected for comparison.

Man of a thousand faces! That was what Benson had become with the shock that killed the flesh of his countenance. Till now, he had used this odd phenomenon only incidentally. Now he utilized it to the full. And the result was something like magic. Anyhow, it left MacMurdie mumbling under his breath.

Murdock had a flat face. Benson massaged his own cheeks and forehead till some of that flat look was attained. It was mainly illusion, for the bony structure under the plastic flesh was unchangeable. But the illusion was startling, artistically good.

Murdock had high cheekbones. Benson massaged the flesh of his face up and forward a little. The flesh stayed where it was left—and he had high cheekbones.

Murdock had a faint cleft in his chin. Benson pressed the tip of his thumb against the gruesomely plastic flesh at the tip of his jaw—and a small cleft appeared.

When the miracle was done, Benson's face resembled Murdock's as a blurred carbon copy resembles an original letter. With the two faces side by side in the mirror there was, of course, no question of telling which was which. But separate the two, and the resemblance would hold!

"Mon, ye ought to go on the stage!"

Benson didn't answer. He stripped the ancient pants and sweater from Murdock's unconscious body and donned them. They were too big for him.

"Your height and your eyes," said MacMurdie, "are what will give ye away."

Murdock's eyes were muddy brown. Benson narrowed his pale-gray eyes sleepily, to minimize the difference. Later, in a life destined to be perilous and active as the lives of few men ever are, he would have a dozen pairs of shell-thin eyeball glasses, with different-colored pupils, to slip over the telltale gray flames in his dead face. But he had no such thing now.

Later, he would have dozens of pairs of shoes, with varying thickness of soles or with no soles at all, to change his height. But he could only bear himself on tiptoe, now, to reach some of Murdock's slouching stature.

"All we want is to land," Benson said. "This ought to get us ashore. After that—"

He went aft, to the cockpit controls, and slipped the hook from the wheel. The boat, held on its course by the hook, was very near the island.

"Inside, Mac."

MacMurdie hid in the cabin, beside Murdock's still form. Benson sent the boat straight at the low cliff.

There was no hole in sight!

Benson's pale eyes widened a little. There had to be a hole there! The chart showed it. Meanwhile, he didn't dare slacken speed or show uncertainty. It might be noted from the shore and arouse suspicion.

It wasn't until the prow of the fast boat was within fifty yards of the cliff that a rocky knob just off-shore was passed enough to reveal the water-edge cavern. Benson breathed a sigh and sent the boat into it at reduced speed.

Not far back in there was a roughly leveled rock ledge. There was a mooring ring in it. Benson brought the boat to a stop and moored it. There was a sound of steps.

He looked around and saw a crude stairway, cut in the rock, leading up. A man appeared at the foot of these, a bald-headed, paunchy fellow with a gash for a mouth.

"Took your time, didn't you, Murdock?" snarled the man. "You know we want that insulin fast. And the other supplies."

In the cabin, MacMurdie literally held his breath. Benson calmly straightened up from the mooring ring, and took a step toward the paunchy man.

The man stared pugnaciously at the flat face with the high cheekbones and the cleft chin. The face of Murdock.

"Farr wants to see you right away. He wants to work on Vincent some more, and you're the boy for that, with your little tricks—" The man stopped, then stared, slack-jawed.

"Hey! You're not Murdock—"

Size and eye color had given Benson away. But not till the resemblance had let him get near the man—which was all Benson had asked it to do.

Benson leaped. The man crashed back against the rock cave wall, with hands like a steel vice at his throat. He tore and twisted and turned, and could not break the pressure.

MacMurdie came from the cabin. Benson's eyes held a reflection of Alicia and little Alice, victims of this man among others. The flaming pale orbs also, for an instant, held madness.

But before the purpling unconsciousness of the man could pass into the blackness of death, Benson forced his eager hands to relax their grip.

He laid the man down, and MacMurdie, with rope from the boat's locker and swabs of waste from the same source, bound and gagged him and the still-unconscious Murdock.

Then the two went up the rock stairs.

The stone steps ended in a clump of bushes cleverly concealing them from any chance walker on the ground.

They peered from the bushes at an old house a hundred yards away.

The house was big and rambling. In its day it had been quite a summer estate. But it was boarded up now, with weeds where a lawn had been. A falling-down little sign announced the place as Thornacre Hall. Benson nodded.

"Thornacre. A Buffalo realtor. Died a few years ago, and his estate has been tied up in the courts ever since. This place among the rest of the things—evidently—closed and unused. Nice spot for a hideout."

Benson was still in the old pants and sweater and still wore the amazingly good likeness of Murdock's face instead of his own. MacMurdie shivered a little and looked away.

"House?" he said succinctly.

Benson nodded.

Mac sighed dolefully. "We'll do no good there," he said, pessimism blanketing him with gloom. "They'll be three or four to one, with machine guns and all. We won't get to first base, Muster Benson."

Benson was beginning to understand this sail-eared, huge-footed assistant of his; was beginning to understand that before action the dour Scot was sure always of disaster, but in action was a devil on wheels and equally sure of success, no matter how improbable.

Benson's pale-gray eyes almost smiled in the white, still mask of his face—or, rather, of Murdock's face.

"Come along," he said.

Bushes to tree to stack of underbrush piled long ago by a neat gardner to burn but never fired. Underbrush to low stone wall to the edge of the lawn. And there they paused a moment.

"We're stuck, mon. We could never cross that cleared space without being seen—"

"The weeds are shoulder-high," Benson said quietly. "We'll crawl."

They started. Over their heads as they inched forward

with toes and elbows the weeds waved sinuously, but there was a little breeze blowing to cover that.

And then the breeze suddenly stopped, and MacMurdie didn't! The movement above him was a dead give-away if anybody was looking.

A shout from the house told that someone was.

"Hey! What's that out there in the weeds—"

The wicked snout of a submachine gun poked in that direction. The gunner drew a careful bead—

CHAPTER XVII

Sleet Of Death

In the basement of the rambling, boarded-up house, Smitty lay along the wall as well as his chains would permit, resting a little. Even his gigantic strength had been frayed a bit that night. For hours on end he had stood or sat in strained positions, rasping his arm irons against the wall behind him.

It had chewed on the nerves of the others.

"For Heaven's sake!" Andrews had snapped raggedly. "Stop that infernal noise, will you?"

"What do you think you're doing?" Vincent had put in. "You think you can wear through chains that size? Don't be a fool, man!"

And toward the end, Mrs. Martineau had developed an excellent case of hysterics. But the noise had gone on.

After a little rest, Smitty stood up and turned to the wall. He held the metal band on his left wrist so it would not bite too deep into the flesh and pulled.

His vast back and shoulders knotted and rippled. His arms corded like tree trunks. His huge hands went milk-white with strain.

And the chain link welded to the iron wrist band snapped where the rubbing had worn it thin.

The right chain followed, and Smitty was held only by the leg irons. He stooped down.

Then he straightened in a hurry, grasped the broken ends of the chain and stood with his hands behind him as if he were still confined. He'd heard steps and seen the solid basement door start to open. The gang here had neglected him for a long time. Apparently they were ready to give him their attention now.

Through the basement door came three men. The one in the lead was a powerfully built fellow with a face a little less coarse than the faces of the other two, but even more cruel. He was dressed in a dapper, stream-lined way. He came up to Smitty. The other two stood just behind him.

"So this is the guy you picked off the boat last night," the dapper man said, looking at Smitty.

"Yeah, Farr," said one of the other two. Smitty's muscles tightened. This was the leader here.

"And you don't know how he got on?"

"Nope."

"Well," said Farr, smiling evilly at the giant, "we'll soon find out. Who are you?"

The question was addressed to Smitty. The giant said nothing.

"Not talking, eh?" said Farr. He turned to the other two. "He'll be all right in those chains, big as he is. Beat it up and keep watch with the others. I don't like this guy's presence. There may be others around."

The two men who had come as Farr's bodyguard left. Smitty stared expressionlessly at Farr.

The dapper big man put his hand in his pocket and drew it out with a shiny object in it. The object was a pair of pliers.

Farr grinned. "See these? They'll make you talk. Now—who are you? What are you doing here? How did you get here? Are there any of your pals around near the island?"

Smitty said nothing.

Farr leaned nearer. "You'd better speak up. You've no idea what an ordinary pair of pliers can do to a guy. Still not talking? O.K.—"

Farr reached for the giant's cheek, with the pliers open and their toothed jaws parted.

On the other side of the basement, Mrs. Martineau

screamed wildly. Farr paid no attention. The four men—
Leon was on his feet now—shivered and turned away.
Mrs. Martineau screamed again and collapsed.

The pliers almost touched Smitty's flesh—and Smitty
smiled and whipped his vast right hand around from
behind him.

Farr, with sudden horror in his eyes, tried to leap
back. He was too slow. The hand got his throat. Just one
hand. But it was enough.

Farr was a strong man himself, in a normal way. But
normal strength was a joke when stacked up against
Smitty's gigantic bulk. Farr beat at the iron wrist behind
the huge hand—and didn't weaken the grip in the least.
He sagged with all his weight to tear loose—and was held
firmly upright at the end of one rigid, tremendous arm.

When he really did collapse, Smitty held him up
that way for another thirty seconds to make good and
sure he was out. Then he opened his hand. Farr fell like
a wet sack.

"Good heavens!" breathed Vincent.

"Young man," said Old Ironsides, sideburns bristling,
"that was miraculous. There was only one thing wrong.
You shouldn't have opened your hand so soon. If you
knew what that fiend has put us through—"

Smitty paid no attention to them. He was sitting on
the basement floor, face to the wall. He caught hold
of the chain manacling his left foot, placed his feet
against the wall, too, for a greater brace, and pulled on
that chain.

The others watched him, scarcely breathing, knowing
that they were seeing something they'd probably never
see duplicated again. And the giant's back arched and
strained, and his hands went milk-white again.

The other chains had been weakened by the rasping
of the end links against stone. But these had not been
similarly weakened. But, on the other hand, with these
Smitty was able to get the full purchase of arms and
back, chest and legs.

Two hundred and eighty-five pounds of solid muscles

heaved on the two-foot length of chain. And in the center, a link not brazed at the ends as solidly as the rest, abruptly straightened and let go.

The chain on his right leg pulled free from the wall, taking staple and some of the wall with it. And Smitty was free. He walked to the nearest basement window, trembling a little, for even his almost incalculable strength had been overstrained a bit. But the tremors soon subsided, and he went to work on the window bars.

The whole grating, four bars and an iron frame, ripped loose in its stone sill under his Gargantuan tugging. But before he could give it the final yank that would tear it completely out, there was a cry from one of the men at his back. Vincent.

"That man Farr! Watch out!"

Smitty whirled—and leaped. But he was too late. Farr had come to a little sooner than expected. He had crept to the door while everyone was breathlessly watching the giant's incredible feat of strength. Now he had the door open.

"Everybody! Down here!" he shouted hoarsely, as loud as his bruised throat would permit. "Here! Quick! The big fella's loose!"

Then he was outside and had slammed the door and bolted it, just as Smitty thudded against the panels to follow him. Smitty leaped for the window and completed tearing the bars out. He poked his head out—and instantly fell back in again.

A swift burst of machine-gun fire had almost taken his nose off with its first emergence from the window.

He was free of his chains, but still a prisoner in the basement. He went back to the door, and banged against it with a pile-driver shoulder. Then he jumped warily aside. And it was well he did.

Lead poured through the wood in a solid stream following the impact of his shoulder. A man was posted out there with a machine gun.

Smitty, growling with baffled rage, leaned against the

wall next to the door and waited. There seemed nothing else to do at the moment.

Outside, in the high weeds of what had once been a well-kept lawn, MacMurdie and Benson lay four yards apart after MacMurdie's mistake in waving the weeds when there was no breeze to wave them normally.

Those pale, deadly eyes of Benson had seen the slip. On just such trifles as that, the gray-steel man had staked his life many times in his adventurous past.

"Left—fast!" he snapped in a low tone to MacMurdie, the instant he saw those weeds wave when they shouldn't have been waving.

The two split right and left. Fortunately the breeze was blowing again, covering the weed movements. MacMurdie and Benson had hardly gotten their distance apart when there was a monotonous, terrible hammering as slugs came from a machine gun. The space between them—where they had been lying an instant before—spewed little gouts of dirt where bullets ripped. Weeds fell as if severed by tiny, unseen scythes in the hands of gnomes.

Then the leaden hail stopped. The two could only lie there and wonder if the man were coming, gun in hand, to see if he had hit anything. They couldn't see over the weeds from where they lay, and didn't dare raise their heads.

As a matter of fact, the man was coming. He went slowly, a few steps at a time, gun cradled and ready. He was beginning to think he'd shot at shadows. But he wanted to make sure.

MacMurdie turned his head to stare at Benson. The gray fox of a man could barely be seen through the few yards of weeds. The Scot felt a chill touch his spine. He himself was in mental agony, wondering if the man were sneaking up on them, wondering when he would feel machine-gun slugs plow into his back. He knew his face expressed all this. But Benson's face did not—could not—express anything at all.

It was still, calm, terribly emotionless. The pale and

143

deadly eyes flaming out of the face that was shaped to resemble another man's, gave a ghastly effect. Like eyes peering from the grave. From another man's grave!

And then, at a stroke, he saw the gray man's stony calm shattered to bits.

From the house, high and terrible, came a woman's scream. And Benson went all to pieces. Another scream sounded out, and Benson's face, sweat-beaded, went down to grind into the earth.

A woman in terror—perhaps in torture! Was it—could it possibly be—Alicia? His wife—alive in there? The possibility was too much to be borne. Benson was a quivering and helpless bulk in the grip of an unendurable hope.

MacMurdie watched in growing horror. If the man with the gun *was* creeping up on them, Benson, in his present state, would prove as helpless as a child.

"Mon, mon, get yersel tagither!" MacMurdie begged soundlessly. And then he heard the weeds rustling not twenty feet away. And Benson, still a quivering wreck from that scream, had obviously not heard.

Mac's groping hand closed on a rock the size of his fist. With a flick of his bony, powerful wrist, he snapped it as far to his left as he could. Which, since he dared not disturb the weeds with a full throw, was not far.

It stopped only a few feet away—and hell broke loose and shaved the dour Scot's ear.

The machine gunner poured lead into the spot where the rock had waved the weeds for a full five seconds. Then stood—and watched. He was too old a hand to risk being gripped by the ankles if he went unwarily closer to whatever was disturbing the weeds.

The pause did the trick. There was suddenly a man's faintly heard yell from within the house.

"Everybody! Down here! Quick! The big fellow's loose!"

The man turned toward the house. Benson and Mac followed carefully.

The basement windows were at the sides of the house.

144

And anyone watching the doors from the *inside* would be apt to overlook a stealthy entrance from the *outside*.

Benson waved to the Scot to come onto the porch. MacMurdie did so. He flattened against the wall while Benson tried the front doorknob. The door was unlocked.

With his pale and deadly eyes glittering like ice in a gray dawn, Benson stooped down and got Mike, the special little gun. He coolly opened the door.

There was a man in the front hall, with his back turned. He was watching in the wrong direction, it turned out. He whirled at Benson's entrance.

His gun started to snap up, wavered as he saw the face of Murdock and the clothes Murdock had worn when he left in the motor cruiser.

"Murdock—" he said questioningly.

Then, with its soft, deadly spat, Mike spoke. The man went down, scalp deeply gashed on the top, knocked out, but not killed, by the stunning impact of the little slug glancing from bone.

They went down two steps of the winding stairs leading to the basement. There they halted as a burst of machine-gun fire sounded around the bend beneath them. Somebody shooting through the basement door? It sounded like it—

There were pounding steps in the hall, coming toward them. Men—too many to face, were converging from all the rest of the house to the basement.

A machine gun at the bottom of the stairs, men coming to the top. Benson's pale eyes flamed lambently. He crept to the bend in the stairs, and leaped like a jaguar.

CHAPTER XVIII

The Big Shot

The machine gunner never knew what hit him. He was crouching on the bottom stair, gazing at the door, through which he had just poured a burst of lead at the battering impact of Smitty's shoulder.

Benson lit on his back. His head banged against the door.

"Whitey!" yelled one of the men just starting down the steps. "What's up? Is he getting out—"

Benson had the door bolt open. He flung the door open just as the first of the men got around the bend in the stairs and stopped talking as he saw MacMurdie and the white-haired man with the steely light eyes.

The two got into the basement just as slugs began to rip through the door they'd banged behind them. A huge hand fell on Benson's shoulder. He started to whirl and hit, but stopped. His flashing brain told him there was only one hand that big; and only one "big fellow" the gang could yell about being loose.

Smitty! He'd gotten through!

Benson turned. He stared up into the giant's moon-face with profound gratitude and admiration. But he only said:

"So now we're *all* cooped up in here. But I guess the three of us can take them."

Outside, Farr's savage voice sounded: "Seven of us, with two Tommy guns, I guess we can take *them* all right. All together when I tell you—"

Benson leaped to one of the basement windows. As he moved, he ripped off Murdock's old sweater. He draped

147

it over the window, shutting out nearly all light.

Instantly, without a word said, Smitty went to the other window and shaded that with his shirt. He may have looked as slow-witted as he was big, with his full-moon face and his too-good-natured-looking, not-very-intelligent blue eyes. But actually his mind was as fast as his fists.

The basement door burst inward. The men outside jumped in yelling—and stopped in utter surprise.

They had jumped into blackness. The basement, in spite of a little light still leaking in the windows, was Stygian in comparison with the outer light. In that completely unexpected blackness, three men waited for them —one a giant who could throttle a man with one hand, another a man with death residing permanently in his flaming, almost colorless eyes, a third with great knobby fists like bone mallets.

"Back out!" one of them yelled, with the utter terror of a trapped animal. "I can't find the light switch—"

There was a stampede, but they were not allowed to get out and scheme all over again. Smitty hit the group.

From the giant's ankles dangled lengths of chain that struck at legs like the death scythes on the wheels of a Roman chariot. On his wrists were the metal cuffs, so that if a sledge-hammer blow of his fist missed its target in the darkness, the metal gyve was apt to slash straight across a face.

Beyond, Benson was at the door, keeping anyone from getting back out. Those pale eyes could see a little in the dark, like a cat's. Methodically his lashing fists downed men escaping from the giant.

To Smitty's left was MacMurdie, battering away with sanguine Scotch howls.

Three against seven. But you could have searched the country over and not have found another three like them. And with the darkness aiding them, and making the guns of the seven useless, they pared odds down—till no odds at all remained, and they alone were on their feet.

Benson went to the windows, white dead face as devoid of expression as a death mask. He took the coverings, and light came in.

All there gasped and looked hurriedly away from him. He lifted his hand to his face and discovered why. A blow in the fight had landed on the dead flesh of his right cheek. The flesh had taken the imprint of the fist, and had stayed flattened, making his countenance lopsided.

He massaged the insensitive, plastic cheek. It came into normal shape—but now one side of his face was in the cast of Murdock, and the other was in the mold of Benson.

"Bind them," he said to Smitty and Mac. He didn't care about his face. In all the world he only cared about one thing now. A woman had screamed. Was it Mrs. Martineau lying in a corner in a dead faint? Or was it—

He ran up to the first floor.

"Alicia!"

He ran through room after room, dim from the boarded windows.

"Alicia! Darling!"

He went to the second floor, the third, the attic. Room after room. And all were empty.

Then, slowly, moving wearily, he returned to the basement. The five kidnap victims crowded around him, thanking him for their delivery, promising him anything he wanted.

He looked at them without seeing them.

Buffalo.

Leon and Mrs. Martineau went to a hospital. Hickock and Vincent went to their homes. Andrews, whose home was burned, went to a hotel.

Benson left Smitty and MacMurdie at the hotel. Then the gray fox of a man with the pale and deadly eyes absented himself, with no word of explanation.

He was gone for over an hour. It was nearly nine in the evening before he came back, as enigmatically as he had left. He sat down near the telephone stand in the room, hand ready to pick up the instrument.

The bony Scot and the moon-faced giant were bursting with curiosity. MacMurdie cracked first.

"If ye don't mind questions, Muster Benson—have ye found out anything?"

"The whole thing," nodded Benson, hand near the phone. "Though a lot of it I've known, of course, for some time.

"Buffalo Tap & Die Works is the stake. Or, I should say, the cash reserve of Buffalo Tap & Die. By a freak of the recession, the total outstanding stock of the company has sunk to a value on the board of about five and a half million dollars. But the company actually has—aside from all its other assets—over fourteen million dollars in liquid cash in the bank! That means that you could buy the company on the stock market for five and a half million, throw the factory buildings and plant equipment away—and still get back fourteen millions by simply withdrawing the cash the company has deposited in the banks. A quick, sure profit of nearly nine million dollars.

"If the stockholders would sell at the present figure.

"The little stockholders could be frozen out easily. But the big stockholders, owning a majority of the stock, were a different proposition. Being in the main sound business people, they wouldn't think of selling. So they were kidnapped and forced to sign 'sell' orders to their broker.

"That is what was behind these kidnappings and murders. Nine million in cash!"

MacMurdie whistled.

"Whoosh! Nine million dollars! Armies have been slaughtered for less than that. But who is the mon behind—"

The telephone rang. Benson snatched it up. A voice said quietly: "They're there. They just went in. Their private office."

Benson hung up, and rose, pale, deadly eyes flaming coldly.

"Come on. It's the last act. We've got them."

In the fast roadster, Benson drove toward the business district.

Both MacMurdie and Smitty stared at the dead, white face. Benson stared straight ahead, with words slipping from his almost moveless lips like slow, deadly knives.

"As you said, Smitty, they are rich, powerful, respected. They could hire brilliant legal talent, drag out a trial for months—perhaps even get off in the end by shoving all the charges on the cheap gunmen who did their dirty work for them. No, they will not be arrested."

"Ye mean to kill them?" said MacMurdie, with entire approval in his harsh Scotch voice.

The deadly pale eyes flamed and dulled.

"No. I'd like to, with my bare hands. I'd like to watch them die slowly under my fingers. But . . . I'm no executioner."

"If ye don't kill them, or have them arrested," said MacMurdie, perplexedly, "what will ye do?"

"They'll get justice done to them. You'll see. At least, I think you will. It's on the slight chance that things won't work out as planned that we are on our way to their office now."

"I wonder," said Smitty, "if Carney and Buell have any idea what's happened to their plans?"

The ground-floor offices of the brokerage firm were dark. So was all the rest of the office building at this time of night. All but one office, high up. That was the private office of the partners.

They sat in there, waiting for a third member to show up.

Buell leaned back in the swivel chair at his desk, gimlet eyes glittering with the greed of a miserly man about to acquire great stacks of additional gold to fondle and count.

Carney, at his own rosewood desk, a heavy-set man with a country-club complexion, dreamed of a bigger yacht and a twenty-acre estate for sale for only seven hundred thousand dollars.

"Tonight should see the end," Buell said contentedly.

Carney nodded. "They'll be getting that last signature at Thornacre Island about now. We ought to get the 'sell' order before closing tomorrow. Then . . . we're done."

Doubt shaded Buell's acquisitive face for an instant. "If anyone ever found out our part in this—"

"Nobody will find out," said Carney easily. "Even the thugs who did the actual work for us don't know our connection with it. And the rest is all perfectly legal.

"We own Tap & Die, to the last share of stock. It cost us five and a half million. We liquidate the company, getting what we can for plant and equipment, and drawing out that juicy fourteen-million-dollar cash reserve. Who's to say anything about that? It's our company. We can break it up if we want to."

"If any of those people taken to the Island should squawk—"

"They won't. They'll be scared to death to say anything. They're promised sure death if they do. As for the financial transaction—we're working through a dummy set-up. Our names are kept completely out. So is *his*."

Buell seemed reassured. He looked at his watch.

"By the way, shouldn't *he* be getting here pretty soon?"

Carney nodded, smiling with thin, pale lips.

"Any minute. And you know, the fact that he's coming whispers to me that they've got that final signature—Vincent's—right now. I don't think he'd be coming here if they hadn't. He told us he wouldn't put in a personal appearance till the end."

Buell nodded, eyes glittering. "Say! If he has—we can complete the deal tomorrow!"

He opened the top drawer of his desk. There were cigars in there, and he was an inveterate smoker. He reached for the flat, expensive box.

"We've got to be careful, though, Carney. If by any

chance an investigation were called, there are loopholes—"

Buell stopped. He stopped abruptly, and he stared into the desk drawer as if he had seen a poisonous snake there.

What he saw, as a matter of fact, was as deadly as a reptile.

Over in the right-hand corner, beside the flat .38 automatic he habitually kept in his desk since the cashier's cage had been held up four years before, were two things—a letter and a postcard.

The letter, on a flat, unfolded little sheet of paper, was from Mrs. Robert Martineau. It said simply "This is to authorize you to sell my Buffalo Tap & Die stock at the current quotations."

The postcard was from Isle Royale, Thousand Islands region, and said: "Insulin. Fast." And was signed Murdock. There was a P.S., and at this Buell stared with his eyes glazing with horror and despairing fury. It said: "Everything going well, according to your orders."

For five seconds Buell glared at that damning postcard. Then he satched up the gun and leveled it at his partner.

"You dog!" he panted. "You double-crossing rat!" His voice rose to a scream. "No chance of anything going wrong, eh? Our names kept out of this, eh? I can see now why you're so sure everything will be all right! You—and *him!*"

"What on earth are you yelling about?" snapped Carney, getting to his feet so fast that his chair tipped over behind him, but standing very still before the death in Buell's maddened eyes.

"You know what I'm talking about!" screeched Buell. "'Everything going well, *according to my orders!*' So you and *he* planned to frame me for this, did you? You were going to turn *me* over to the police to take the whole load so that if investigations did start, you'd be in the clear!

"Or maybe you meant to kill me and then have the police find me!" raved Buell. "That postcard and the 'sell' order in my desk—and maybe beside it a 'suicide' note from me!"

"I swear—" mumbled Carney hoarsely, staring at the gun muzzle with wide, horrified eyes.

And then there was a noise at the door. Steps—and a hand on the knob.

"The police!" yelled Buell, utterly mad. "This is them now! You called them to get me! You planned—you and *he*—"

The gun bucked and trembled in his hand. Planted evidence! Police to pick him up! Well, they never would—

Carney fell, bleeding from four or five wounds, any one of which would have been fatal. Buell, still screaming, broke for the opening door. He emptied his gun into the dumbfounded figure appearing there, leaped over it, and raced down the corridor.

A figure that seemed to tower clear to the ceiling stepped around a corner, caught him by the nape of the neck and held him up with one hand like a kitten.

Smitty carried the raving man back to the office, followed by Benson and MacMurdie.

Carney was dead. Near the door, the other victim of Buell's madness was lying unconscious.

The third member of this murder firm. The third who was going to split something over nine million dollars in viciously acquired cash.

"Why, look—" stammered MacMurdie. "Why—"

The man who lay there, arms sprawled, bullet holes dripping crimson, was Lawrence Hickock. Old Ironsides.

Benson stepped to the office phone and dialed police headquarters, pale, deadly eyes playing like cold flame over Old Ironsides' stark form. The man at the head of the trio! The man, more than any single person, responsible for what had happened to Benson's wife and child!

"Buell & Carney's office," Benson said into the phone, immobile lips barely moving with the words, face utterly dead. "Hickock came here, as I said he would. You can come and get him and the other two rats."

CHAPTER XIX

Three Against Crime

In the hospital, Hickock lay dying. At police headquarters, Buell, a gibbering wreck, was listening to his talk with Carney, from a dictograph planted in their office by Benson. Then he raved a confession. But Benson was not there to listen. He was at the hotel. The gray man already knew the main outlines, if not the entire details, of the murderous affair.

It had been Hickock's plan. Buy Tap & Die stock, and loot the big cash reserve. If anybody refused to sell under threat—take him to Thornacre Island and make him sell, by torture if necessary. It had been necessary with all save John Lansing, who had discreetly surrendered and sold with the first threat of death.

It was Hickock who had thought up the clever scheme of carrying the victims to the hideout in an ordinary transport plane, whose regular trips would not arouse the possible comment that the frequent appearance of a private plane might have done.

But in the actual kidnappings lay the greatest risk of eventual detection. The dummy Tap & Die set-up *might* be penetrated at some future date, and the names of the men actually profitting be discovered. So Hickock acted in advance to kill any possible future suspicion.

He had taken the hazardous "kidnap" trip himself, with not even the gangsters knowing he wasn't the victim he seemed to be. That is, all but Farr, leader of the gang. To Farr, Hickock had appealed secretly when he found himself running out of insulin which, as a diabetic, he must have—

"That nailed him," said Benson, staring at the hotel-room wall with pale eyes in which was no triumph but only a great weariness. For after all, the main goal had not been accomplished. A gang had been mopped up, and their crafty, undercover leaders nabbed. But no trace had been found of Alicia and little Alice. "The call for insulin put the finger on him at once."

MacMurdie shook his Scotch head. "I don't see—"

"The gang didn't care anything about the health of its victims," said Benson. "Once they got the signature on the 'sell' order, nothing mattered.

"But when Hickock needed insulin—that was different! Immediately a hurry call went out. Why the solicitude for *his* health? What did they care whether Hickock had medicine or not? The only possible answer was that Hickock had a tie-up with the crooks."

"Well," said MacMurdie somberly, "the mon paid for it. And so did Carney, and so will Buell. Thanks to you, Muster Benson."

The gray fox of a man stared at the wall.

"Ye didn't want to kill them yourself because, as ye said, you're no executioner. Ye didn't want them arrested because they might buy their way out with their power and their money. So ye arranged for them to eliminate themselves." '

Still Benson said nothing. But the Scot, knowing the genius now of the pale, steely figure, was sure in his knowledge of what had really happened.

"When ye planted that dictograph, ye also planted a duplicate letter you had Mrs. Martineau write, and the postcard with a little additional message on it which ye wrote yourself. Planted it in the desk of the partner that also had a gun in it, which happened to be Buell's.

"Ye knew when the two had got to their office, Muster Benson. Ye knew that Buell would go wild when he saw he'd been framed. And ye knew about when Hickock would come scurryin' to tell of the slip in plans. Knowing all that, ye made their fates for them." The Scot's bitter blue eyes flamed. "So crooks kill crooks, and it's perfect justice."

Still Benson said nothing. The man who had moved super-criminals to their own destruction, like a master chess player moved pawns and rooks, could not feel the grim elation felt by Smitty and the Scot. He had only one thought in mind.

"*Could* my wife, my little girl be still alive?" he said at last.

Smitty stirred, and his eyes took on a great pity. He'd have liked to encourage Benson's hope, but in justice he couldn't. It is no favor to encourage a delusion.

"They were dropped from the plane over the middle of Lake Ontario," he said, as gently as possible. "I was dropped, too. Same place, same way, for the same reason. And I was dropped without a parachute—as far as they knew."

Benson stared at him, gray eyes terrible. But the giant went on.

"Is it likely that . . . they . . . had parachutes put on them, any more than I did?"

For a second it looked as though the steely-gray figure would flash on the giant. And if it had, Smitty would have stood still and taken all Benson cared to give. But finally Benson relaxed.

"I suppose you're right. But I will always hope—"

Then MacMurdie reluctantly voiced what both he and the giant were thinking.

"The job's done, Muster Benson. Me and this over-grown chunk of muscle here have helped as well as we could. So now I suppose we'll be sayin' good-bye and good luck to ye."

"Oh, no," said Benson quickly.

The Scot stared. Benson went on more slowly, face dead and immobile but pale eyes flaming like ice in the dawn.

"I've been thinking it out, Mac, Smitty. And it comes to something like this: I've suffered a terrible loss. But

157

others have suffered as greatly—and still more are doomed to suffer in the future. You two are cases in point. You, Mac, lost as much as I have. You, Smitty, spent a year in jail on a false charge. Now, having suffered myself, I would like to help others in the future."

The two were still, hardly breathing, as they listened to the slow words slip from the dead lips.

"There is much work to be done that the police can't handle. I'd like to do that work. I'd like to devote the rest of my life, and my fortune, and what talents I possess, to fighting crime of the sort that has made my own life barren and meaningless. I'll need help. Would you two . . . like to stay on with me and administer justice—our way?"

Smitty's vast shoulders, swelled exultantly. "Of course, chief!"

MacMurdie's bitter eyes burned blue flame. "With the greatest of pleasure, Muster Benson."

"Right," said Benson. "You, Smitty, will be a personal assistant. You, Mac, will have a nice drugstore in payment for your help." He held up his steely, slim hand as the Scot would have protested at the inactive course suggested. "It will be a special kind of drugstore, Mac. It will be equipped, as no drugstore ever was before—to fight crime. We'll settle in New York, I think. As that's the biggest city, it is frequently the headquarters for criminal activities as well as more legitimate enterprises."

The pale-gray eyes ceased to focus on the two and stared through them.

"You can go now, if you don't mind, and leave me to work out the rest of it."

Gently, the two left, almost on tiptoe. For they knew that the thoughts he wanted to be alone with were not of the future.

They were of the past: of a woman with tawny-gold hair and brown eyes, and a little girl who was her image.

On into the dawn the steel-gray man with the pale and deadly eyes sat with his thoughts. Roused by the loss of all that made life worth living, he had been a terrible force. But he had still been a man.

Now, he was hardly human. He was a shining, sinister machine. An engine of destruction, forged unwittingly by crime, created by an underworld which henceforth was destined to shudder at mention of the thing he had become.

The Avenger!